BASED ON TRUE EVENTS

Believe

Her pretty eyes hid a million lies

A novel by

ABHILASH

Be*lie*ve

Copyright © 2024 Abhilash

Publishing year: 2024

About the author

Abhilash's debut novel, The Rural Banker, was published in 2020. He wrote Believe entirely on his smartphone. He writes and talks about pro-wrestling for a living. He graduated from Symbiosis International University in 2016. Abhilash runs a food vlog on Instagram, @abhilashfoodie.

: @abhilashmonty

Disclaimer

This story is based on real events. Names have been changed/altered to protect anonymity. Certain details have been slightly modified to ensure a seamless reading experience.

Introduction

"Things come apart so easily when they have been held together by lies."
- Dorothy Allison

What's your biggest fear?

Loneliness? Being broke? Failure? Rejection?

Here's what I fear the most.

Imagine being betrayed by that one person you trust with your life. A betrayal that leaves you broken and turns your life upside down.

Imagine.

A person comes into your life out of nowhere, convinces you that you're destined to be together forever, showers you with the utmost love and affection, and then suddenly leaves you, never to return, no matter how much you beg and plead.

You're now a shell of your former self. There's absolutely nothing to look forward to in life. The one who betrayed you is living life to the fullest while their memories and their broken promises torment you every single day. They don't care one bit and have moved on.

And one day, you depart this world after going through immense pain and suffering for years on end. While taking your last breaths, you wonder how your life would've turned out if they had kept their promises. You're miserable, full of regrets, and in tears. And then, you're forgotten. Like you, the tragic and harrowing story of your destruction is lost in time, erased forever.

That's the fear that plagued my mind for two straight years.

The fear that resulted in the creation of B*elieve*.

On June 4, 2009, I failed 12th grade on what was the darkest day of my life. Little did I know that I was going to feel its repercussions for years to come.

Academically, it came as a boon to me. The ordeal humiliated me to such a degree that I vowed to never fail a subject again, let alone an entire year. Fortunately, that's exactly what happened.

My personal life is what my academic failure ended up affecting. It led to someone coming into my life. A woman. I'll address her as Lieshaa throughout this book. Her arrival completely turned my life around. For the better.

Or so I had thought.

It's quite interesting that my perception of the biggest failure of my life has changed twice over the years. Back when I failed 12th grade, it was hands down the worst moment of my life. Almost a decade later, I realized that I wouldn't have met Lieshaa if I hadn't faced that academic setback. The worst moment of my life had miraculously turned into the best.

It's 2024 now. I'm back to square one, regretting the day I failed 12th grade, wondering where my life would be today if I hadn't met her.

Writing this story required me to browse through thousands of texts that were exchanged between Lieshaa and me over five years. It wasn't easy for me to read those texts since most of them were utter lies and the one who had sent them had moved on, never to return.

The texts featured in this story haven't been modified so as to keep their authenticity intact. The characters who appear in this story are based on real people and their names have been changed/altered to protect anonymity.

Love makes a person commit the most evil and unforgivable deeds. I committed one six years ago and paid a heavy price.

Be*lieve* chronicles a series of events in my life that took place over the course of 12 years, between 2012-2024. An emotional rollercoaster full of twists and turns from beginning to end, it's a heart-wrenching story of three individuals, entangled in a web of love, betrayal, and deceit.

It's an account of how a bored housewife stuck in an unhappy marriage destroyed three lives with her lies. How she used her deceased mother to manipulate the one she desired into loving her back. How karma caught up with a man who betrayed his friend's trust. How a fairytale love story turned into a living nightmare.

It's a harrowing tale of a dangerous and evil woman who disguised herself as an innocent and troubled soul to quench her lust.

Years down the line, Lieshaa and I will have ceased to exist. The millions of thoughts, feelings, and memories housed in our minds are going to fade away into nothingness.

But Be*lieve* will still be around. This story will never die, serving as a cautionary tale about how lies destroy lives.

Contents

Part III: Lieshaa Leaves

Behind Believe

Prologue

Place: Somewhere in Central India.

Date: February 8, 2024.

Time: 1:45 p.m.

"I love you so much.. I can't live without you.. My dear mom… I swear on you. I love Abhilash so much... you're my god as well... please make my wish come true... please make sure Abhilash and I are together forever.. I love you n miss u..."

I read the text message out loud on my phone while staring at Lieshaa, not taking my eyes off her for even a second. My eyes were piercing hers while she was sobbing uncontrollably. I could sense that she was ashamed and the last thing she wanted to do was to lock eyes with me.

Her husband Rahul, my former best friend, was sitting on the couch a couple of feet away from where she stood. All he did was stare into nothingness while I read the message that his wife had sent me six years ago. I could only imagine the barrage of emotions running through his mind at that very moment.

The tension in the room was so thick that one could cut it with a knife. There was utter silence in the room after I finished reading the text message. I could swear that it lasted an eternity.

Their daughter hadn't returned from school yet, and thankfully so. At nine years old, she wouldn't have had trouble understanding what was going on and I certainly wouldn't have been able to utter even a single word in front of her.

I put the phone in my pocket, got up off the couch, and headed towards the gate. Lieshaa didn't move an inch from her spot, and neither did Rahul.

The distance between me and her home was steadily growing with each step I took. The woman who once said she couldn't imagine living without me was now breathing a sigh of relief, knowing I was finally out of her sight.

After holding back tears for the past hour or so, I finally gave up and broke down. I was a crying mess and didn't even bother to wipe the tears off my face. I had stopped caring a long time ago.

I suddenly paused in my tracks and looked back one last time. The home that had held a special place in my heart for the past several years stood before me. The home that housed the woman who had convinced me we were soulmates.

The past six years flashed before my eyes in a span of a few seconds while I stared blankly at her home. I resumed my walk, reminiscing about that fateful day that now felt like a distant dream.

August 3, 2018, 11:45 p.m.

I was lying on my bed and casually browsing the web on my phone when I received a notification on the Facebook app. It was a friend request! My eyes lit up when I read the name on the notification panel.

It was Lieshaa, the wife of my friend Rahul. I hadn't seen Rahul since 2014 when he bid me goodbye as I was leaving home to pursue an MBA at a prestigious institution in Pune. I had met Lieshaa only once back in 2013, but we never talked and I didn't even know her name.

In fact, this was the very first time that I had seen her face, and she was beyond beautiful.

I clicked on 'Confirm' and resumed browsing the internet.

12:24 p.m.

The Facebook Messenger bubble popped up on my screen. Lieshaa had sent me a message. I quickly clicked on the bubble.

"Hey... remember me??"

I started typing a response. I wish I knew what I was getting into. The destruction of my life had begun at that exact moment.

Looking back now, I wonder what I would've done if I had the slightest idea of what was about to come.

Maybe I would've blocked her immediately. Or maybe, I would've kept talking to her and avoided doing the things that I did. The ones that I now deeply regret.

None of it matters now. It's too late.

Lieshaa and my story didn't begin on this day, though. This tale goes way back to the mid-90s when my family shifted to the city from my birthplace, which was a small town about 40 km away. And it took A LOT of time, roughly 17 years, for the stars to align.

I won't go that far back, for now. Let's start off this story at the place where I stumbled upon Lieshaa for the very first time.

Part 1
Lieshaa's Love

The Stars Align

"I wish I had never met you." - Rahul, 2024

My family moved to the city in 1996. Lieshaa and I first met in 2013. It blows my mind to this day that for the entirety of those 17 years, the distance between our respective homes was a measly two km!

And what's more, we almost came across each other on multiple occasions during this period. But that's a story for another chapter.

In mid-2013, the stars aligned and we finally met. At that point, it had been a few months since I became friends with Rahul. As for Rahul, I met him for the first time in mid-2012.

I began pursuing Electronics Engineering in 2010. The college was about three km from my home. In June 2012, the fifth semester kicked off. I was 21 at the time.

Mere weeks before the semester started, an old friend of mine, Samay, contacted me on Facebook. I was shocked to the core when he told me he was studying at the same college I had been attending for the past two years! Samay and I used to be classmates and the best of friends back in the early 2000s when I was a student in fifth grade. He left the school in eighth grade and we ended up losing contact.

Samay told me that he failed his second year of college and thus had to miss a year. He was now going to start the fifth semester and was beyond excited to meet me after all these years.

I still vividly remember that day as if it were yesterday. The first lecture was about to begin and students were entering the class one after the other. I usually was the first to enter the class and had already made myself comfortable on a desk near the window.

Suddenly, my focus shifted to the door. He had put on a bit of weight over the years but I immediately recognized him. This was the first time since 2004 that I had seen Samay. He wasn't alone, though.

Another guy, roughly 26-27 years old, bespectacled, accompanied him while he entered the class. This was the first time I saw Rahul.

An hour passed. Samay came over to my desk immediately after the professor left the class. We hugged each other and spent the next few minutes reminiscing about our time as classmates in school, almost a decade ago.

Rahul didn't leave his bench, though. Over the next few days, I noticed that he kept to himself and didn't even talk with anyone except Samay, unless absolutely necessary. At this point, I was convinced that he was incredibly shy, timid, and non-confrontational.

Boy, was I wrong!

A few weeks passed. One day, something happened that disturbed me to my very core. A guy named Ishan used to share a desk with me. We had known each other since the first year.

The class consisted of about 60 students and we had been separated into three groups for practical sessions. Samay, Rahul, and Ishan were in the same group and were desk buddies in the practical lab. On this day, Ishan did something that left a bad taste in Rahul's mouth.

Mere days before this incident, someone in my class (who shall remain unnamed) had told me that Rahul had a girlfriend and that she was absolutely stunning.

"Mere words can't express how insanely beautiful she is," the classmate in question had told me. The topic was quickly dropped and I didn't even bother to ask him her name.

This was the first time that I had heard of Lieshaa.

The trio was chilling in a corner of the practical lab that day. Suddenly, Ishan mentioned Rahul's girlfriend while cracking a joke. Rahul was furious but decided against doing anything about it. The ever-mischievous Samay later spoke with Rahul about the incident while the duo was in the college parking lot.

"Don't you think he went too far in the lab? I mean, I would never let someone speak about my girlfriend in such a manner."

"Hmm," Rahul retorted, before starting his bike. Samay's remark was the only thing on his mind for the entirety of his ride back home. It had lit a fire in him that kept him awake all night.

The clock struck one. It was our lunch break. Me and Ishan were having lunch at our desk while Samay and Rahul were quietly sitting at theirs. No one else was in the class. This was a common sight during lunch breaks, as most of the students preferred getting some air for a few minutes rather than being cooped up in the class.

Suddenly, Rahul approached our desk, grabbed Ishan's glasses, and went back to his spot. Confused, Ishan went over to his desk and asked for his glasses. To my horror, Rahul grabbed Ishan's tie. The situation had escalated quickly and I went over to their desk to diffuse the same.

"I've been nothing but nice to you since the day we met. Who in the blue hell do you think you are, cracking jokes about my girl?" Rahul asked him angrily.

"It was just harmless fun. I didn't mean-"

"SHUT YOUR MOUTH!" Rahul was furious. "Keep my girlfriend's name out of your mouth, you hear me?"

"Yeah… I made a mistake and won't ever repeat it. Can I please have my glasses back?" Ishan pleaded.

Rahul finally returned his glasses. Ishan and I went back to our desk. A few seconds later, Rahul and Samay left the class. Ishan seemed okay and had resumed eating his lunch despite what just happened.

I, on the other hand, was TERRIFIED.

While Rahul was yelling at Ishan, Samay and I were doing our best to calm him down. What scared me was that Rahul didn't even look at either of us, as if we simply didn't exist. His sole focus was on letting Ishan know that he had committed a big mistake and that he would be better off never repeating it.

The incident left me shaken. A classmate later told me that Rahul wasn't someone to be messed with. He was apparently a hothead and had a dark past.

"Rahul once barged into a guy's home and beat him up after he caught him staring at his girlfriend a couple of times," he said.

Rahul had seemingly quit his old ways to focus on his career and turn his life around. Not entirely, though, judging by what happened with him and Ishan.

"I need to keep my distance from Rahul going forward," I said to myself while getting into bed that night.

Little did I know that the two of us were only going to get closer in the coming months.

The Book

"Can I borrow a few books for my wife?" - Rahul, 2013

In late 2012, about three weeks after Rahul almost beat Ishan up, he got married to Lieshaa in a temple. He was 26 while she had turned 20 in September.

Rahul and Lieshaa had been together for a long time and were madly in love with each other. Their parents didn't approve of their relationship, though, and the lovebirds decided to have a secret wedding in a temple. A bunch of Rahul's close friends, including Samay, attended the wedding. After the wedding, Rahul and Lieshaa began living together in a small room on the terrace of his parents' home.

As for how did Rahul and I become close friends?

It all started when the college authorities made a massive error while creating the attendance list for the sixth semester. It's common knowledge that these lists are in alphabetical order.

Not this time, though.

The attendance list that was created for the sixth semester was a big, randomly generated mess. My name being Abhilash, I always used to get one of the earliest roll numbers. This time around, though, I got the 40th roll number. Thus, I was put in the final practical lab group. Thankfully, Samay was still in the same group.

And so was Rahul.

My friendship with Rahul kept growing with each practical session. He even invited me to a small dinner party that he threw at a restaurant to celebrate his wedding with Lieshaa.

One day, Rahul's bike broke down and Lieshaa ended up dropping him to the college on her moped. She also came back to pick him up in the evening. She saw Rahul waiting by the college entrance gate, stopped her moped, and waved at him. While sitting on the pillion seat, Rahul pointed at the far corner of the college parking lot.

"That guy beside the yellow bike is Abhilash. He's the one I was telling you about that day. We're in the same practical group along with Samay."

After failing in my 12th boards in 2009, I made myself a promise that I would never fail a class again. So far, I had passed with flying colors in every semester and didn't want to break the streak. The fear of failure had turned me into an ideal student who could do no wrong and was the apple of every teacher's eye. I never missed a class, was always the first to complete journals, and submitted assignment copies on time.

Rahul used to borrow my practical journals often. I learned years later that he used to give my journals to Lieshaa to copy the content in his books.

"The lean guy who's talking with Samay, right? Lieshaa's eyes sparkled with curiosity.

"Yeah, that's the one," said Rahul, before asking her to turn the moped. He didn't have the slightest idea what was going on in his wife's mind.

The sixth semester included a mandatory mini-project submission. It didn't take long for Samay to find a professor who used to make projects for engineering students at his workshop.

Over the next two weeks or so, Rahul and I paid several visits to the professor at his workshop, keeping ourselves updated on our mini-project's progress. Summers in my city are extremely brutal and unforgiving. On one insanely hot day in April, Rahul and I visited the professor to enquire about our project. We had a quick chat with him, requested a bunch of changes, and exited the workshop.

We chatted outside for a while as I was inserting my bike's key into the ignition.

"Where's your bike, Rahul?" I asked.

He pointed at a coconut water kiosk on the opposite side of the road. There it was, parked on its central stand, right in front of the kiosk. Lieshaa was sitting on the bike, sipping coconut water. She was looking at us. I couldn't make out her face, though. She was too far.

"See ya tomorrow in college," I said, as Rahul began crossing the road. I started my bike and rode off.

The mini-project was a huge success. Our teacher did point out a couple of mistakes but was satisfied with the work we had put in over the past several weeks. That weekend, Samay called me and told me to get ready ASAP. Rahul was elated with the outcome of the project and wanted to give us a treat. After an hour or so, they arrived and I welcomed the duo to my home.

Rahul had never been to my home before. While I was passing him a glass of chilled water, I noticed that he was staring at the massive shelf that stood in a corner of my room.

"I store all my comic books and novels in there. Wanna see?" I excitedly asked and opened the shelf even before he could respond.

Rahul's eyes gleamed with surprise as soon as I opened the shelf. He gaped in astonishment at the 4000+ books that were neatly placed in there. Five of the six columns were filled to the brim with nothing but books that I had bought and collected over almost a decade.

"HOLY SHIT! Have you read all of these books????" Rahul couldn't believe his eyes, while Samay had already started browsing through the shelf. He was aware of my obsession with reading comic books and novels. I fondly remember occasionally lending books to him back when we were classmates in school.

"Yep, I've even read a small portion of this collection twice!" I exclaimed, enjoying the attention my bookshelf was getting.

"My wife... she LOVES reading comic books and short stories! Any chance I could borrow a few books for her?" Rahul asked expectantly. "I'll make sure to return them in a few days."

11 years later, his words still ring in my ears. Looking back now, I wonder how different things would be today if Rahul had never come across my bookshelf and hadn't borrowed a bunch of books from me on that fateful day.

"Of course! You can take as many books as you want. I used to lend books to the kids in my colony before smartphones became easily accessible," I said while taking out a few books.

I was surprised, to be honest. I had never met a girl at that point who was into reading comic books. I was aware that Lieshaa had quit college after her wedding to Rahul. I could not imagine spending day after day, cooped up in a small room. I was glad my books were going to help kill her boredom.

Rahul took a few comic books, a novel, and a book collecting stories of ghost sightings and poltergeist activities from all over the world. Being a horror fanatic, the last book held a special place in my heart.

At that moment, I had no idea that this book would one day become my most prized possession.

Rahul, Samay, and I then enjoyed dinner at Al Zam Zam, a favorite restaurant of mine. He returned the books about a week later. I put them back in their respective spots on the bookshelf.

I sometimes wonder. What if I had a time machine? What would be the first thing I would do?

I would've traveled back in time to this very moment and uttered a single word while my past self was putting the books back on the shelf.

"STOP!"

That Damned Smile

"I used to come with him to see you and only you, but you wouldn't even look at me." - Lieshaa, 2018

It had been a month or so since the seventh semester started. I was lending books to Rahul regularly at this point. He used to always return them in a few days, browse through the bookshelf, and pick new ones for his wife.

It was the second week of August. Rahul was absent that day but had informed me that he was going to meet me behind the college during the lunch break. He needed to submit an assignment in a day and had planned to work on it at his home, using my notebook.

As soon as the clock struck one, I stormed out of the classroom, the assignment copy secured in my hand. I walked past the gate and was about to call Rahul when I noticed a moped in the distance.

He wasn't alone, though. I could make out a figure sitting behind him on the moped. It was Lieshaa. The girl I had heard so much about over the past few months. There she was, inching closer with each passing moment.

Rahul stopped the moped right beside me. For the next minute or so, we talked about a bunch of stuff, including the assignment deadline.

Being an incredibly shy and reserved person, I made it a point to put my complete focus on Rahul. Even though I didn't look at her at all, I could make out her outfit. She was wearing a red top, coupled with black knee-length shorts.

While my eyes were locked with Rahul's, I noticed from the corner of my eye that a big smile had formed on her face. She was the wife of the guy who had become a close friend of mine over the past six months or so. My introverted self felt that I would make Rahul uncomfortable if I glanced at her for even a split second.

After the duo left, I went back inside the college premises. I still didn't know what she looked like. I hadn't looked at her even once. All I remember about her from that day is that smile of hers.

That sweet, beautiful, damned smile.

The next couple of months were pure hell. The results of the sixth semester had come out. A bunch of students had failed in the previous year, including Samay and Rahul. It meant that they had to wait another year sitting at home and couldn't attend classes anymore.

Every single day felt like an eternity. My best friends had suddenly stopped showing up and I hadn't felt this lonely in a long time. I used to spend days upon days without having a proper conversation with other students.

Now that he didn't have much to do, Samay used to visit often to binge-watch TV shows with me. He came unannounced one day. He was attending a call and signaled for me to listen closely, before turning the speakerphone ON.

Lieshaa was on the other side of the phone. She seemed distraught and in a state of panic. I had never heard her voice before.

She was complaining about Rahul and it was clear as day that something had happened between them. She was urging Samay to talk to her husband ASAP.

That voice of hers. I could hear that soothing, melodious voice all day and not get tired. It carried a certain charm that I feel to this day, 11 years later. Suddenly, it dawned on me that I was breaching her privacy.

"They fought over some trivial issue," Samay told me after cutting the call. "She's been calling me incessantly since the morning, asking me to talk to Rahul about it," he chuckled.

I let out an awkward laugh, before quickly changing the topic. I didn't feel like wanting to know more about the couple's private issues and found it odd that she was discussing it with Samay. I didn't think much of it, though, and the incident was out of my mind in a few minutes.

Samay wasn't the only one who used to occasionally visit me. Rahul hadn't stopped borrowing comic books from me and used to come by to get new books at least once every two weeks. On that day, while I was taking out a new batch of books for him, my mom called me from the living room.

"Why don't you ask the girl to come and sit inside as well?"

Lieshaa had tagged along with Rahul this time around! And she was outside!

I ran outside the house but she was nowhere to be seen near Rahul's bike. I began looking in every direction and finally found her. She stood quietly about three houses away from mine. She had her face covered with a scarf. A bunch of kids were playing right in front of her and it seemed like she was enjoying watching them play.

"Maybe she's too shy to come inside," I mumbled to myself and decided against asking her to come and sit inside. I went inside and noticed that

Rahul had picked up a few books himself. We walked to the gate while I told him about my day in the college. He started the bike and sped past the kids, finally stopping beside his wife.

Lieshaa sat on the bike and immediately looked behind, right where I stood. I instinctively smiled at her, though I was pretty sure she was too far to even notice.

What was going on in my mind at that very moment?

Rahul had become one of my best friends by that point. As for his wife? If Rahul could somehow peek into my mind, he wouldn't have found even a single thought about his wife that would make him uncomfortable. I wasn't the kind of guy that Rahul would have to worry about. I wouldn't dare.

The bike took off and disappeared around the corner of the last house on the block.

I wouldn't see Lieshaa again for the next five years.

Farewell, My Friend

"I never felt as helpless as I did on the day you left." - Lieshaa, 2018

On December 15, 2013, I wrote an MBA entrance test held by a prestigious international university. My brother was pursuing a BBA in the same university at the time and I was determined to pursue my MBA in one of its institutions. Back then, it seemed like the perfect next step in my academic career.

A day later, the eighth and final semester kicked off and brought good news with it. The students who had failed the third year were being allowed to attend the final year classes! The order had come directly from the university. My best friends were back and I couldn't be happier.

At this point, I had grown close to Rahul to the point that we could joke around with each other.

Or so I thought.

It was the first week of January. Samay, Rahul, I, and a few others were chilling out in the classroom on our lunch break. I suddenly cracked a joke and ended up mentioning Rahul's wife.

Even though I can't recall what the joke was, I clearly remember it being a completely harmless one. Everyone laughed at the joke, while Rahul simply smiled.

"You've changed quite a bit over the past few months, Abhilash!" he said, still smiling.

"Wait, really?" I asked, surprisingly.

"Yeah, quite a lot, actually."

I immediately realized that he didn't appreciate me bringing up his wife while cracking a joke. Rahul didn't grab my tie or threaten me, though, seemingly because he had way more respect for me than he had for Ishan.

But that smile, coupled with his cold demeanor, sent chills down my spine. I knew at that moment that this was the first and last time I would bring her up in front of Rahul.

February 28, 2014.

The big day was finally here. Samay kept assuring me all day in class that I was going to get selected. Two weeks ago, I traveled to Pune for the admission interview and it went incredibly well. I still had my doubts about clearing it, though.

"You're clearing it without a shadow of a doubt," Samay said, as we were heading home in the evening. I loved how casual his demeanor was, as if he knew for a fact that I was going to receive good news in a matter of hours. I smiled at him before we parted ways outside the college.

It was 7 p.m. and the time had FINALLY come. I filled in my credentials and kept staring at my phone's screen with bated breath.

"You are selected for MBA - Telecom Management. Click here for your call letter."

I couldn't believe my eyes. I had done it! I was going to Pune to pursue an MBA at one of the most esteemed universities in India!

I treated Rahul and Samay to dinner that night. I couldn't help but feel that this was, hands down, the greatest moment of my life.

The reality of leaving home for the first time hadn't set in. But it was about to, in a few weeks.

May 31, 2014.

It was three in the afternoon. The bus was scheduled to leave at 3:30 p.m. Rahul helped me load my suitcase in the cab. Samay was vacationing in Kashmir and hence couldn't come. I took one last look at my home, somehow managing to hold back my tears before the cab took off.

Rahul had accompanied me and my parents to the bus stop. He parked his bike at a corner while I waited beside the bus.

"What a journey, huh?" It was all I could come up with, while we embraced. This was way harder than I had expected.

"Yeah, and I can't thank you enough for your help over the past two years or so. Let's keep in touch while you're there," Rahul replied.

We hugged each other one last time and I wished him the best of luck for his future. I then climbed inside the bus with a heavy heart, while Rahul headed towards his bike.

At that very moment, at Rahul's home, Lieshaa was lying on her bed, staring blankly at the ceiling.

There were tears in her eyes.

Career Woes

"I had lost all hope of ever seeing you again." - Lieshaa, 2018

The reality had finally set in. The pursuit of a good career made me write the entrance test in late 2013. I was beside myself with joy when I got selected for an MBA. In all the hullabaloo, I forgot that I had to leave my home and family to pursue higher studies, something I had been dreading for a long time.

One of the absolute worst moments of my life was finally here. Two days after arriving in Pune, my parents were minutes away from bidding me goodbye at the hostel, situated on the top of a hill.

The walk from my hostel room to the parking lot seemed never-ending. While my parents were getting in the car, I finally noticed that my mom was an emotional mess. The heart-wrenching sight was my breaking point and I finally broke down in tears as well. We wiped the tears off each other's faces before they took off. Later, my mom told me that my father began weeping as soon as the cab took off and cried all the way to the hotel.

A long, unpleasant journey had just begun. I was the one who had signed up for it but was now having second thoughts. At this point, though, it was too late to turn back.

If I begin writing about those four years, this book will end up having twice its intended page count. Instead, here's a quick rundown of some of the most notable moments that happened between 2014 and 2018:

• I scored 3/15 in one of the subjects on the first internal exam, thus failing it. It made me realize that homesickness wasn't the only issue I was dealing with. I actually had to study as well to survive two years of my MBA.

• I lost contact with Samay. He and his older brother had opened a restaurant back home while I was dealing with an insanely hectic schedule. I used to call Rahul on Saturday evenings without fail, but that didn't last long. We ended up losing contact as well.

• Lieshaa, at this point, was just another person that I knew and had never interacted with. I forgot her like I had forgotten many others in the past. She wouldn't pop up in my mind for the next several years. Looking back now, it's funny as hell, considering how I can't go an hour without thinking about her.

• My MBA consisted of a whopping 48 subjects, with half of them being in the second semester alone. Those were arguably the most grueling and demanding five months of my entire academic career.

• I spent the months of April and May 2015 in my hometown for my internship. I also somehow managed to survive both semesters without failing a subject.

• I tried calling Rahul upon reaching my hometown. The number didn't exist anymore. I learned years later that he and Lieshaa had left his parents' home and had rented a room on the outskirts of the city.

• While I was pursuing the third semester in Pune, Lieshaa and Rahul welcomed their first child, a daughter. The birth of their daughter led to them shifting back to Rahul's parents' home.

• In one of the most heartbreaking moments of my life, I failed to bag a job on Day 0 sometime in October 2015, along with about 40 other students. Three months later, I finally landed a job at a big IT company in Pune.

• Now placed, I could care less about scoring in the final semester. I had the time of my life during the last three months of my MBA.

• On April 20, 2016, I departed the campus the same way I had arrived on it in 2014- in tears. The last few months had brought that place closer to my heart more than the previous three semesters ever did.

• I lasted a total of six months in IT. It didn't take long for me to realize that I just couldn't get used to an IT job. I returned to my hometown in late 2016. Directionless, I decided to prepare for government bank exams.

• After studying for about a year, I cracked the IBPS PO prelims in October 2017. A month later, I passed the mains exam as well. In January, I traveled to Pune for the final stage of the selection process. The interview went way better than I had expected.

• On the morning of April 1, 2018, I found out that I had bagged a seat in a government bank! I had put the bank in the first spot on my priority list as it had hundreds of branches spread across the state, and I didn't want to move to a different state. I later found out that a whopping 8.30 lac students had enrolled for the exam, about 3500 seats were filled, and my rank was a respectable 944.

And thus, this four-year ordeal finally came to an end, and I couldn't be happier. I started counting down the days until I got my posting.

Vani's Reluctance

The countdown had begun. In a few months, I was going to get posted in a bank somewhere in Maharashtra, India. I spent the better part of April collecting documents that I needed to submit to the bank officials at the city's main branch.

My daily routine for about three straight weeks was getting up, driving through the city in unbearable heat, collecting documents, and hitting the bed. Over those three weeks, I paid multiple visits to the nearby police station, a hospital (for a health certificate), administrative offices, and numerous photocopy shops.

The whole ordeal was incredibly tiresome, but I at least had someone with whom I could talk about my day. I met Vani on a dating app in the first week of April, mere days after I got placed. We instantly hit it off and began talking every day, as and when my hectic schedule permitted.

During the last week of April, my brother and I decided to go on a short trip to Dubai. I had gotten my passport way back in 2014 but hadn't traveled outside India yet. I was aware that I wasn't going to get another chance to travel abroad for a long time after being posted.

I kept in touch with Vani while in Dubai, showing her every notable tourist attraction via video calls. We did the desert safari and visited the Dubai Mall and the Dubai Frame. The absolute best part of the trip was being able to watch the entirety of Dubai from the 124th floor of the Burj Khalifa.

Since a lot of Indian people traveled to Dubai via Sharjah Airport, it had a restaurant that served ready-to-eat Indian cuisine. We had a *dosa* and *pav bhaji* before heading towards the boarding area.

As we were boarding the plane, I wondered if I would ever come back here. "Probably not," I murmured to myself. I wasn't a big travel buff and also wasn't a fan of long flights. The only reason I agreed to the trip was to use my passport at least once before starting my demanding government job.

I was dead wrong. I was going to come back here somewhere down the line, in the midst of what I now consider the worst year of my life.

A month had passed since our Dubai trip. Vani and I weren't together anymore. She knew that there was no way I was going to get posted in my hometown, and she wasn't sure about having a long-distance relationship.

"You knew from the very beginning that I was going to leave the city, right?" I asked her.

"I did. But now that I've fully processed the situation, I think that long-distance relationships aren't my thing. Your workload will keep increasing with each passing week. It's better to end things now than to let the relationship die a slow death over several months," she said bluntly.

I pleaded with her to give this thing a chance but to no avail. That was when she said something that left me dumbstruck.

"Can I say something? What if you don't go at all?" She was dead serious. "I have strong feelings for you and you are aware of that. You're too talented and can bag any job here in the city itself. It doesn't matter if the pay is bad, at least we will be together and manage somehow. What do you think?"

"Are you out of your goddamn mind? That's one of the most absurd things I've ever heard, to be honest with you. I paid a hefty amount to pursue an MBA, bagged a job in IT, left it, studied for a whole year, finally landed a government job, and you want me to quit it? I think we're done here," I angrily said before hanging up.

The fact that the relationship didn't even last four months helped me get over it pretty quickly. In mid-July, I learned that I had to travel to Bangalore on August 18 for two weeks of training, before finally getting the posting. The days were passing by pretty quickly now, and I was excited to begin this journey.

August 2, 2018, 11:15 p.m.

I turned off my mobile data, switched off the phone screen, and put it beside me before closing my eyes. My life was going to change FOREVER in a matter of hours.

Part II
Lieshaa's Lies

The Return

August 3, 2018, 12:24 p.m.

"Hey... remember me??"

It had been five long years since I last saw Lieshaa. I was experiencing a barrage of emotions. It had been such a long time. How was she? What had she been up to all these years? How did she find me? I had so many questions!

This was also the very first time that I saw Lieshaa's face. One quick look at her profile picture made me realize that she was pretty as hell. Also, I realized that Rahul had never brought her name up back in the day, and I never asked as well. If I hadn't noticed her last name in the friend request tab, I wouldn't have realized that she was the wife of my friend.

"Mere words can't express how insanely beautiful his girlfriend is," the words my classmate uttered six years ago were ringing in my ears. He couldn't have been more right.

She had sent a picture of Rahul as well. He was holding a baby.

"OMG, hii! Congratulations on having a baby!" I responded excitedly.

"Thank you so much... are you married??"

"Haha, nope! I'm about to join a government bank in a week or so. How's Rahul?"

"Wow, congratulations Abhi! Rahul works as a lecturer in a nearby college. You're crazy about gym and fitness, right? Me too!" she wrote, before sending me a picture of herself in workout attire.

"Home gym? That's impressive!" I wrote. Her gym outfit was only adding to her beauty and charm.

"Abhi, do you have a recent photo of yours on your phone? Actually, I haven't seen you in years," she wrote.

I sent her a couple of photos, before telling her how Rahul used to come to my home all the time back in the day.

"Yeah, that was the last time I saw you... Abhilash... I need to pick up my daughter from her playschool. Bye, and take care..."

"Yeah, sure. Bye, Lieshaa! And it was the seventh semester if I remember correctly."

The message wasn't seen. She had already gone offline. Lieshaa... a person that I hadn't met more than once, way back in 2013. Someone I had completely forgotten about, to the point that I hadn't thought of her even once since leaving the city in 2014. Out of the blue, she had come back into my life.

And somehow, she didn't seem like a stranger at all, even though this was the very first time that we had talked with each other. I was also quite excited about finally meeting Rahul again after four long years.

Lieshaa came back after an hour or so and we resumed our talk.

"You remember everything, huh? Do you remember my face??" she asked expectantly.

"I kind of did, Lieshaa. The only time I saw you up close was when you and Rahul took an assignment copy from me behind the college, remember?"

"Woah! You do remember!" She seemed happy that I hadn't forgotten her. "Can I get one more picture of you? You haven't changed one bit in the past five years, Abhilash. You also must've made a ton of new friends over the years."

"Not many to be honest, Lieshaa. I have always been a bit of an introvert. Even back then, I used to hang out with just two of my classmates, Rahul and Samay."

"Hmm... well, I'm your friend now. Wasn't before, but I am now!"

"That's so sweet of you! Yeah, you certainly are!" I responded.

I then told her about my trip to Dubai two months ago. She seemed ecstatic. This was also the first time she asked me if I had a girlfriend.

"Woah! Dubai? Did you go with your girlfriend? It's such a wonderful place, must have been a dream come true, right?" She asked.

The excitement in her messages was quite evident. Over the years, I've realized that this is usually the case in the early stages. This was our very first talk. She was getting excited about anything and everything that I was sharing with her.

Imagine a person who just met you and is talking to you in a manner that makes you feel like the most important person in the world. Now, fast forward two years later, and that person is talking to you in the same manner. Nothing has changed. They are still the same. They still find you interesting.

They are the kind of person you should never let go. I wish Lieshaa was that person.

"LOL, nope! It was me and my brother." I replied.

We kept chatting for a while before I took Rahul's phone number from her.

She again asked me if I had a girlfriend. This was the moment I realized that maybe, just maybe, she was into me.

"Abhilash, what's your girlfriend's name? It's been five years. You're good-looking. I'm sure many girls must want you."

"I did have one about a month ago, but she ended things and we aren't together anymore."

"WHAT?? That's sad. She left you... how could a girl in her right mind leave someone like you?" she asked.

"The same way you left me a few years later, you treacherous, lying, sorry excuse of a woman," my future self mumbled under his breath while reading this message of hers in 2024.

I explained what had happened between Vani and I.

"Ah. Don't worry Abhi... I'm sure the prince will get his princess soon..."

Our talk ended on a sad note when Lieshaa told me that her mom had passed away from cancer three years ago. I was heartbroken when she revealed that her dad was also battling cancer. A few months down the line, he would pass away as well.

The next day, Lieshaa messaged me in the morning. She asked me what I was doing. When I told her that I was chilling on the terrace, she brought up the time she accompanied Rahul to my home back in 2013.

"Yeah, I remember Abhi... I've seen your home once. I was waiting for Rahul in front of a house at the end of the block while he was inside. I saw you when you came outside with him. Your eyes... it felt as if your eyes were trying to say something... that was the last time I saw you."

Lieshaa then pleaded with me not to tell Rahul that she was texting me. She further said that even though he wouldn't have an issue, she wouldn't feel like messaging again if he found out.

I assured her that I wouldn't say anything to him. I wish I had.

That weekend, Lieshaa took things even further while talking with me.

"Abhi... I wanted to say something..."

"Sure, Lieshaa. What happened? I asked curiously.

"Actually, I've never talked with a guy the way I talk to you. Except one person, and he's my husband now. I'm scared sometimes, but I can't help but talk with you."

"Lieshaa, that's incredibly sweet of you. And if you ever feel like you can't talk with me or if you're scared, we'll stop talking right away. No hard feelings at all. I completely understand," I assured her.

"Okay. Then let's stop talking right now, okay? For good."

I could sense she was angry at me. I told her that I was simply trying to do what was best for her.

"Why? What happened? It doesn't matter to you anyway, so why even bother talking?" she wrote.

"Okay, I apologize. It does matter. I didn't mean to hurt you and I'm truly sorry," I tried to diffuse the situation.

"Abhi, what would you have done if I wasn't married? Would you have married me? Be brutally honest," her next question came out of the blue.

"Lieshaa! I'm speechless! I... I probably would have. You're one of the nicest people I've ever known. But that doesn't matter. You're married to my friend."

"Abhi, I love your eyes, your hair, your lips... what I'm trying to say is that you're perfect! What I love the most about you is your nature. That's all I wanted to say. Good night!"

She went offline before I could respond. My eyes were fixated on her last message. Rarely had anyone ever talked to me in such a manner and thought so highly of me. On the other hand, I kind of knew what she was up to. I had to do something to make her understand that nothing could happen between us, and I had to do it ASAP.

The next night, Lieshaa asked me if I talked with other girls as well. I assured her that I didn't. She made me promise her that if I ever found someone, I wouldn't stop talking with her. When I promised her, here's what she responded with:

"I wish I was single... I... I'm also scared of losing touch with you once you leave the city, Abhi."

"Lieshaa, you shouldn't say such things... I know friends lose contact with each other all the time. Hell, even Rahul and I lost contact after I went to Pune. But I promise you, we'll always remain friends."

"But I don't consider you a friend, Abhilash."

I didn't know how to respond to that text. I decided against writing anything and simply waited.

"Not a friend... Not even a god... if there's something in this universe that holds a higher status than a god, that's what I think of you. You're such a simple guy. It's hard to find someone like you nowadays. I like you Abhi, I'm not kidding. Feels like I should keep talking to you and do nothing else all day." she wrote.

"Lieshaa, don't compare a mere mortal to God, please..."

I quickly changed the topic and reminded her about my time in engineering and the friends I made back then. I brought up Samay and her tone completely changed.

"To this day, I don't know how he got my number, Abhi. He used to text me sometimes. I rarely responded. Maybe he liked me. Maybe not. I don't know."

I knew she was lying. My mind immediately wandered back to 2013. Lieshaa's fight with Rahul wasn't the only time she had called Samay. Samay and I were the best of friends back then and he once showed me a call log noting how often she used to call him. She likely gave him her number and for some reason, was ashamed of telling me the truth.

Unfortunately, this was the first of a long, long list of lies that Lieshaa was going to tell me over five years.

I didn't mention this to Lieshaa. I didn't want her to know that I knew she was lying, thus leading to an awkward situation.

"Abhi, we should sleep now. It's too late. I know you're gonna come in my dreams anyway."

"Aww, that's so sweet of you to say! Good night, Lieshaa, sweet dreams!" I wrote, before turning off the mobile data.

The next day, I could sense that she was feeling low. She told me that she had a fight with Rahul and hadn't talked with him all day.

"Abhilash, can I get a hug? Friends hug each other all the time, don't they? After Rahul, you'll be the first guy that I would hug. I swear on my baby."

"Lieshaa, you don't need to swear on your kid. I believe you," I said, before sending her a GIF of two people embracing each other.

"Abhi, there's a guy. Lives in the neighborhood. He somehow got my number and has been bothering me for a while now. I'm fed up at this point."

"You should block him immediately, Lieshaa. Or else, maybe tell Rahul? God, some guys..."

"He... he's a friend of Abhay. Maybe I should ask Abhay to tell him to back off."

"Who's Abhay, Lieshaa?" I asked. She had never mentioned the name before.

"My childhood friend. Still lives beside my parents' home. He's like a brother to me. He did propose to me once, to tell you the truth."

"Woah! Really? What did you say to him then?"

"I rejected him, Abhilash. But we remained good friends. He still visits us sometimes."

"Ah... got it!"

"Abhi, what happened? Are you worried for me?"

"Yeah, I am... have you blocked that guy? Abhay's friend?"

"Abhi. I... I apologize. I lied. There's no guy. I just wanted to see if you would be worried about me if I said that someone was bothering me. I'm truly sorry, Abhi. Abhay did propose to me, though. And I did reject him, Abhi. I swear on you."

35

I hated it when someone played such games. I didn't say anything, though. I respected her too much to point out to her that what she did wasn't right. This was one of her several red flags that I was going to ignore in the coming years.

Lieshaa's Proposal

Rahul visited me the next day and brought along his three-year-old daughter. The last time I had seen him was at the bus stop while boarding a bus to Pune in 2014. We spent a few minutes reminiscing about our college days before he took his leave.

It was funny.

The last time he met me, I was about to leave the city. Four years later, he meets me and I'm about to leave once again. I didn't tell him anything about what had happened between Lieshaa and me so far and felt guilty about it. I knew about his hot temper and didn't want to see her get in trouble.

Lieshaa was getting agitated with each passing day. In a few days, I was about to leave for Bangalore for my training. She finally decided to do what she had been wanting to for a long time.

"Abhilash, I need to ask you something very important. Do... do you love me?" she wrote.

"Lieshaa, it's not right and you know that. You're married. To my friend."

"Ok... sorry. But then we shouldn't even talk to each other. It's wrong as well, isn't it?"

"Talking, I feel, is harmless, Lieshaa. But if that bothers you, we can stop it. I've no issues whatsoever, even though it would hurt a little," I was blunt in my response.

"I love you so much... I can't live without you..." she finally confessed.

I was stunned.

I had figured on the very first day that she was into me, but never in my wildest dreams did I imagine that she would speak her mind.

"You're married and you will have to live without me for the rest of our lives. But if you ever need me, I'll always be there for you no matter what. I promise you, Lieshaa."

And that's when Lieshaa sent the text that sparked something in me. The words that ring in my ears to this day.

"My dear mom... I swear on you. I love Abhilash so much... you're my god as well... please make my wish come true... please make sure Abhilash and I are together forever.. I love you n miss u..."

I was dumbstruck.

Lieshaa had previously cried a couple of times while remembering her mom during our calls and chats. I knew how much her mom's untimely passing had affected her. And here she was, pleading with her mom to keep the two of us together, forever.

A part of me wanted to say those three words back to her, but I somehow managed to control myself.

"Abhilash, I don't know what you'd think of this. But I've been meaning to say something to you for a long time now. And I'm scared."

"Lieshaa, I have nothing but respect for you. You're hands down the nicest person I've ever come across. You don't need to hesitate one bit. Ask away," I encouraged her. I wasn't prepared for what was about to come.

"Listen. Let's run away together. I've never loved someone as much as you. Not even Rahul. Believe me. I spend my days thinking about how it would feel to wake up every morning and see your face. I sometimes end up crying and wonder why you didn't come into my life sooner. I think I'm going into depression. I shouldn't have gotten married so early. I can't concentrate on anything. I simply can't live without you.

"Abhi. You and I would look so good together. You're so freaking hot and handsome. I spend hours just staring at your pictures on Facebook. And I get worried that those pictures are out there for other girls to see as much as they want. I want to marry you. I... I want a baby from you, a mini version of you.

"Please listen before saying anything. Even if you don't want me, at least give me a baby. I'll raise it as my own. And I would feel like the luckiest woman on earth, knowing that a part of you will always be right in front of me. I'm begging you."

"Lieshaa… wh… what are you… you can't be serious?"

"I am…"

"Listen… this can't happen, Lieshaa. Please understand what you're asking of me. You're married to my friend Rahul. You have a daughter with him! How can I marry you? How can I give you a baby?"

"Please, Abhi… I need it more than anything in the world. I've realized now that I won't be able to live without you. At least give me a baby… that looks just like you. I'm begging you."

"NO! This isn't right, Lieshaa. I can't do this to Rahul. A baby? I would never be able to forgive myself for doing this to him. Lieshaa… please. Not this. Anything else and I will happily say yes. But not this, please. You're asking for something that could destroy several lives at once," I tried to make her understand the ridiculousness of her request.

"Abhi… I know how ridiculous it sounds. But I need a baby from you, a little Abhi who looks just like you. I wish I could tell you how much I love you, Abhi. An adorable baby that we can play with, love, and raise together. Doesn't it sound wonderful?"

Little did I know back then that I was going to regret rejecting her request for the rest of my life.

I spent about an hour trying to make her understand what she was asking of me. She wouldn't take no for an answer, and deep down inside, I had a soft spot for her as well. But there was no way I could grant her wish.

In the end, she called it a night before sending this heart-wrenching message:

"Abhi. When you get married to someone in the future, make sure you don't invite me. I beg you. Don't even let me know. It's a request, Abhilash. My heart won't be able to bear the pain."

In two days, I was going to leave home to start my training 1100 km away. At this point, Lieshaa couldn't stop crying and was begging me to stay.

"Please, don't go. Not even a month has passed and you're leaving me alone, AGAIN. Abhilash, can't you stay? We can meet as much as we want."

"Lieshaa, I've worked incredibly hard for almost a year to bag this job. I can't just stay back and let it slip from my hands. You understand that, right? I promise I'll keep visiting as much as I can. I hope you won't forget me, though."

"Forget you? No... I promise you. I'll be thinking about you till my very last breath. You have no idea what you mean to me. I had never imagined that such a sweet person would ever come into my life," she said, sobbing.

"And Abhilash... if you ever leave me or stop talking to me for some reason, I won't be able to live. I can't help it. My heart... it's too weak."

"Lieshaa. I swear on my mom. It will never happen."

"Abhi... I want to dedicate a song to you. Please listen to it when you can," she wrote, and sent me the song, "Love Me Like You Do." I was familiar with it, as one of my friends in MBA used to blast it on his mini-speaker often.

"I love this song, Lieshaa! Have been listening to it for quite some time now. I'll listen again right away," I wrote back. She had gone offline by then.

It was the evening of August 17. I was packing my bags and my mobile data was off. About two hours later, I turned it on. Lieshaa had sent a lengthy message.

"You're leaving tomorrow, Abhilash. Please take care of yourself. Couldn't talk to you the past two days and missed you A LOT. You were in my mind all this time. Please come back soon. To be honest, I'm a little worried. Please don't start talking to someone else. Remember, you promised me. You won't break it, right? And don't stress yourself out over office work. You're an intelligent guy and can handle the toughest of situations, I know that. I'm with you, always. I'll pray to God every day that you end up coming back to the city soon. I need you the same way a person on their deathbed would need oxygen, Abhi. My heart, my mind, my body, every fiber of my being needs you... I'll miss you so much... you're leaving me all alone here, again. I will always love you. GN. SD. TC."

A tear rolled down my cheek. I couldn't believe that I was crying. I'd never been loved by anyone to such an extent. I knew that if she wasn't the wife of my friend, I would've married her right away. I had started to develop feelings for her and was disgusted at myself.

I was mere days away from making one of the biggest mistakes of my life.

A Secret Unearthed

"Can you at least think about it? I'm begging you, Abhilash," Vani said. She was in tears.

It was the third day of my stay in Bangalore. I was about to doze off when I received a call from an unknown number. It was Vani. I had deleted her number a long time ago.

"You were the one who ended things, remember? I told you we could work things out if we tried, but you were not ready to listen. Why did you come back now, all of a sudden?"

"I made a mistake, okay? I haven't had ONE good sleep since that day. All I'm asking for is one chance. I haven't known you for long, but the one thing I know about you is that you're not heartless. I still love you," she pleaded.

"Well, it's too late now," I replied. "I'll be brutally honest. I don't have feelings for you anymore. I'm hanging up the call now, I have to get up early for my training session. Please don't call me again."

"Wait, ple-"

I hung up.

She begged. She pleaded. She shed tears. I didn't care one bit. "I have someone else now. Someone new, someone who cares about me like no one ever did," I mumbled to myself.

When a person who used to be close to you once, suddenly cuts ties and isn't even ready to listen to you, it hurts. It hurts like hell. That feeling of helplessness is absolutely brutal and it leaves you messed up in more ways than one.

I was that person.

Vani came back, begged, and asked me to take her back. At that point, the only person who was in my mind all the time was Lieshaa. In just under two weeks, she had proved time and again that she could do anything for me and cared about me with all her heart. She had a hold over me, and escaping it was the last thing on my mind.

There's a popular saying about karma.

It is a bitch.

You treat someone like trash, and the same thing just might happen to you someday. I was going to learn this lesson somewhere down the line.

August 22, 2018, 12:10 p.m.

"You're online!"

"You lied to me..."

"Don't ever talk to me again."

"Are you asleep?"

"Are you talking to someone? You aren't awake, right?"

"I guess you're really asleep. Sorry, good night. I love you."

I missed every single message that Lieshaa had sent. I had hit the bed more than an hour ago. The training schedule was quite demanding, with students having to attend classes from 9 a.m. to 6 p.m. I wasn't getting much time to respond to her messages.

After 11 days of intense training, I came back home for a two-day stay. I was posted to a small village, about 170 km from my hometown, and had to report to the bank on Monday.

I rushed to the hospital immediately after my plane landed. While I was in Bangalore, my mom caught a fever and it turned out to be jaundice. As soon as I entered the hospital room, I broke down in tears. Mom was lying on the bed and had lost A LOT of weight. She requested me to stop crying and was having a hard time speaking.

My brother and aunt consoled me but it took a while for me to stop crying. Thankfully, Mom got discharged a week later and steadily regained her health over the next month or so.

Lieshaa messaged me on Sunday evening. It had been a few days since we last talked.

"Abhi, you forgot me… I knew it. I've been yearning to talk to you but…"

"I'm so sorry, I tried my best Liesh. But the schedule was too hectic and I just didn't get time to respond to some of your messages. But the training is finally over and I'm back home. Unfortunately, I have to leave on Monday morning. Since the bank is not more than 200 km away, I'll be coming home almost every weekend!" I wrote.

"I missed you so much. All I could think of was where is he? How is he doing? Is he eating properly? Is he getting enough sleep? Is he okay?"

I told Lieshaa about my mom and she spent almost an hour consoling me. I didn't utter a single word and kept listening to her, wondering how incredibly lucky I was to have someone listen to me when I needed them the most.

"Liesh, should I give you some comic books and novels before leaving? I know Rahul works all day and you get bored up there in that small room on the terrace. I remember... you loved reading books. Rahul used to borrow them for you all the time."

I was scared. She was seemingly spending a lot of time thinking of me. I was on my way to start a new job and didn't want her to keep worrying about me every single day. Maybe reading some novels would keep her occupied.

"Abhi... oh my god!"

"What? What happened?"

"Abhi... I remembered something. I was going to tell you a while ago but it somehow slipped my mind."

"The suspense is killing me now. Just tell me already," my curiosity was at its peak.

"You're in your room, right?" she asked.

"Yeah, I am. Tell me."

"Abhi. If you remember, you once gave me a book… a ghost story or something. I don't remember well but it was probably a collection of stories of real-life ghost incidents."

I didn't bother responding and immediately opened my bookshelf. The book was safely tucked in the middle of a stack of books in the last row of the third column from the top. The last time I had touched it was the day Rahul returned it to me, five years ago.

I carefully took it out of the stack, cleaned it with a cloth, and opened it.

On the very first page, something was written with a sketch pen. It was a cell number. Lieshaa had written it. Five years ago.

FIVE YEARS AGO.

I sat down on the floor right beside the bookshelf, staring at the book, "World-Famous Ghosts." My mind suddenly traveled back to that fateful day. Rahul had returned the stack of books, and I quickly put every book back in its place on the shelf. This particular book, containing Lieshaa's number, stayed in the same spot for FIVE FREAKING YEARS!

"You saw it, I think," a new message had popped up.

"Liesh... I... I don't know what to say. You've been in love with me all these years... why didn't you say anything back then?"

She called a few seconds later.

"I have a lot that I need to get off my chest. I was scared, Abhi. I feared you would reject me, but somehow gathered enough courage to write my number in the book. I saw you for the first time in the parking lot of your college and immediately fell in love with you. Rahul used to hand over your practical journals to me to complete his journals. I used to hold those journals in my hands, feeling as if I was holding you, Abhi.

"I used to accompany him to the college sometimes. I used to put on makeup and wear the nicest clothes in hopes that you would notice me. The boys in your college... I remember so many of them staring at me in the parking lot once. But you... you didn't look at me even once, Abhi. WHY?" she was almost screaming at this point.

"Liesh, you were Rahul's wife. I couldn't... I didn't want to make him feel uncomfortable. I also didn't have the slightest idea what was going on in your mind."

"Abhi. I have been in love with you for five years. I saw you up close behind the college once. I was so close to you, all I wanted to do was hug you as tight as I could. But you didn't even look at me once. It hurt like hell, Abhi.

"I even confessed to a friend of mine that I had fallen in love with you. She consoled me and told me that if Abhi didn't even look at you, he probably wasn't interested in you. Do you remember the project workshop where you used to meet Rahul?"

"I do Liesh... I do," I exclaimed.

"I once asked Rahul to take me with him. I knew you would be there. I was sipping coconut water and looking at you the whole time. It was about 40°C but I didn't care, Abhi. I just wanted to see you. Two years after writing my number in your book, I changed it. For a long time after that, I kept wondering if you ever saw the number and called me, only for a random person to answer it.

"We are poor. After months' worth of saving, we somehow managed to buy a cheap smartphone. The moment I got my hands on the phone, I searched you on Facebook, and sent you a request."

A storm had broken loose in my mind.

I last saw Lieshaa in 2013, then left the city with a heavy heart a year later. I left my IT job and came back to my hometown in 2016. I spent five long years having no idea that right next to my bed, inside the shelf, was a book in which someone who loved me dearly had written her number.

Every big moment that I was involved in during those five years flashed before my eyes in a matter of seconds. My MBA selection, leaving home, being homesick, bagging and leaving a good IT job, spending the next year or so preparing for government exams, my Dubai trip, and much, much more... all this while, the book was right there, a few feet away from me.

Lieshaa was in love with me. She had been in love with me for the past five years. She waited for me for five years. And now, she was back in my life.

She also had a kid with Rahul now.

But the only thing I could think of was that this woman loved me like no one ever did. This was the stuff that dreams were made of. The perfect love story, if you will. And I couldn't hold back anymore.

"Liesh, can I say something?"

"Yeah, Abhi. Please do."

"I think... I'm in love with you as well."

"I Quit!"

It had been a week since I started working and I was missing Lieshaa terribly. I was posted to a far-off village almost 200 km from the city. One look at the village would make you feel as if you had time-traveled back to the 60s.

Almost everything I had heard about my government job was a plain lie. I quickly learned that a banker's job wasn't sitting behind a desk and chilling all day. The bank used to be packed with villagers, EVERY SINGLE DAY.

I was living in a small apartment in the nearest town, 25 km away! The road connecting the village and the town was full of potholes and uneven surfaces. One couldn't exceed the bike's speed above 15 km/hr even if their life depended on it.

It didn't take long before the harsh reality of working in a government bank slapped me across my face. Although my coworkers were incredibly helpful and friendly, the higher-ranking officials sitting in the main branch 60 km away were assholes of the highest order. Most of them talked rudely, were extremely entitled, and always made us feel as if we were beneath them.

The bank's demanding schedule was coming in the way of Lieshaa and me.

"This was bound to happen. We haven't talked in two days. This will keep happening more often until the day comes when you'll be too busy to even answer a message," Lieshaa was unhappy over the fact that the frequency of our talks had drastically reduced.

The day I learned that she had written her number on my book and had been in love with me for ages, I couldn't resist any longer. When I finally told her that I loved her as well, she couldn't believe her ears. She spent the next several minutes crying her heart out, thanking me repeatedly for finally uttering the words she had always wanted to hear.

"I've never felt so helpless. I can't talk to you even though I want to. Abhi... how did this happen? I used to love talking to you, and now I'm lonely as hell. Everything has changed.

"I sleep every night thinking that tomorrow will be the day we finally get to talk. But we don't. If this had to happen, why did we even meet in the first place? I can't stop crying 'cause... never mind, just forget it. Good night..."

"Liesh, I wish you could see what I have been going through here," I wrote, before explaining how insanely grueling my schedule was.

"No... Abhi, I can't see you like this... you're the sweetest person I've ever known, and it pains me to see your suffering. I wish... I wish I was with you, I would have hugged you and taken you away from all of this, someplace far away, where no one else would be there... just the two of us..."

"The fact that you're saying all of this is more than enough to lift my spirits, Liesh. I can't appreciate it enough," I replied.

That night, I didn't sleep until 3. A lot was going on in my mind, and all of it revolved around Lieshaa. Never in my wildest dreams did I imagine that I would fall in love with someone I had completely forgotten about for four years, but here I was.

I was alone, wasn't eating properly, was spending two hours on the road every day, and the higher-ups were starting to get on my nerves.

Most importantly, I was missing Lieshaa. I couldn't bear being away from her. I couldn't bear hearing her cries or reading her messages explaining how everything had changed between us.

I wondered what would happen if she simply gave up and lost feelings for me. It sent chills down my spine. I had never loved anyone as I loved her. I couldn't lose her at this point.

I had finally made a decision.

People do the most idiotic things when they are truly in love. I was about to do one.

Five days had passed since that fateful night. I was back home. Again. I was unemployed. Again. I had lasted a month.

I recalled the conversation that I had with Vani that led to our breakup, mere weeks before I met Lieshaa. She had asked me to stay with her in my hometown instead of leaving to start my career as a banker. And I had rejected the idea since it was the most asinine thing I had ever heard.

Why did I do it for Lieshaa, though?

There were a million reasons, but the one that immediately came to mind was that I could do anything for her.

Quitting my job was a tiresome process. The officials in the main branch did everything in their power to make me stay, but I didn't budge one bit.

"Are you sure you're okay?" Lieshaa asked. "I still can't believe someone tried to attack you and almost succeeded. I wish nothing but the worst upon that person, Abhi."

Yes.

I didn't tell her that I had come back for her. I didn't want her to feel indebted to me in any manner. All I could think of at the time was that she was happy because I had returned. Nothing else mattered to me. Not even my uncertain future. Love tends to make a person take the most drastic decisions. I had taken mine and was going to look back at it with nothing but regret in my eyes.

I told both Rahul and Lieshaa that an angry customer tried to attack me and almost grabbed my neck before a bunch of people caught him and prevented him from hurting me. I further told them that I called HR and quit the job right there and then. I didn't want to lie to her, but telling her that I quit my job for her would've hurt her even more.

The next day, Lieshaa seemed a bit off. She had a fight with Rahul but didn't want to talk about it. She finally caved in after I pressed her for a few minutes.

"We were out shopping. I saw some really pretty bangles in a shop. I love bangles and can't get enough of them and Rahul knows that. I didn't even ask him to buy them for me. All I said was that the bangles were pretty, and he ended up giving me a lecture."

"Lieshaa... how could someone say no to you? I would've... this isn't right."

"Abhi, I wish I could tell you everything I face daily. Raising a baby, being cooped up in a tiny room all day, never-ending fights with him, some of which ended with me being slapped on the face hard, absolutely no support from his parents...I go through so much. I hate how his parents don't give a shit about our well-being. My parents raised me like a princess. Never said no to me, no matter what I asked for. And now... every day brings a new struggle with it. What did I do to deserve this, Abhilash?"

I had no answer to her question.

The next day, Rahul called me. He was now working in a small firm and didn't have a laptop of his own. I gave him my old laptop and he couldn't thank me enough for the help.

He was grateful to me and had no idea what was going on in my mind. I wonder what he would have done if he knew about my sinister intentions. All I could think of at that very moment was to get another job soon, save some money, and take her away from him.

"Abhi, why did you give your laptop to him?" she messaged me that night.

"He needs a laptop for his office work, Liesh. I already have a new one I bought earlier this year. Please understand... if he's happy and busy working, he won't lash at you so often. Hopefully."

"But a laptop... I wish you were here Abhi, I would've showered you with kisses and hugs. I want you to know that I'll love you till my last breath. How did I find someone who's so considerate?"

"Liesh, I don't know if you'll believe me, but I can't think of anything that I won't do for you. I really can't."

"My sweet, sweet Abhilash... you're gonna make me cry. I want nothing from you. Well, there is one thing..."

"Yeah, Liesh?"

"Don't ever leave me."

October 1, 2018, 12:00 a.m.

"Abhi, what's going on?"

"Ordered pizza from my favorite foot truck I once told you about, Liesh.

"Hey, we've been ordering from there occasionally since you told me about it back in August! I love it!"

A new pizza cloud kitchen opened up near my home in May. I was a frequent buyer and once mentioned it to Lieshaa as well.

"Abhi, it's raining. Can you please take a quick look outside? I want both of us to look at the rain at the same time before calling it a night."

"Why not, Liesh. Yeah, it's beautiful outside. The cool breeze flowing through the window, the sweet sound of raindrops, and talking to you... I wouldn't trade this for all the money in the world."

"Oh god, don't make me blush. You say the sweetest things, Abhi. Anyways, it's too late, should we sleep now?"

"Yeah, Lieshaa. I'll be waiting for your call tomorrow."

"Hey, why would I sleep, huh? There's a special person that I'm missing right now. Since it's his special day, I wish I could be with him at this very moment. A very, very happy birthday to you, Abhi! I pray for nothing but the utmost happiness and prosperity for you and your family. Every single day, I wake up and thank God that I have you. I had never imagined that someone as special as you could ever come into my life. But now that you have, you and only you will have a place in my heart till I breathe my last... Abhi."

"Thank you so much, Liesh! I thought you forgot..."

"Abhi... that's impossible, please believe me!" she assured me. "Also, I wanted to give you something... something special, just for you."

"Lieshaa, your presence in my life is the biggest gift I could've asked for. I have that. I don't need anything else from you."

"Shhhh... I won't take no for an answer. Here it is..."

It was a picture of her, in front of the mirror, in lingerie.

I couldn't help but gape at her spotless, white skin. She possessed a well-defined, toned body. I couldn't take my eyes off her pretty face. She was blankly staring at the mirror. There was a sense of calmness on her face. She certainly didn't need to smile at the camera to look pretty.

Lieshaa and I had grown incredibly close over the past few days. We had become so comfortable with each other that talking dirty with each other had become a regular occurrence. We used to spend hours on end talking about what we would do to each other upon meeting. But I wasn't expecting that she would send such an intimate picture of hers. The fact that she trusted me so much meant the world to me.

I was so engrossed in the picture that I didn't realize she had sent another message.

"How was the gift, Abhi?"

"You're hands down the prettiest woman to ever walk on this earth, Liesh. How can someone be so flawless, so perfect?"

"No idea... Abhi. Can I... is it possible for you to send me one? A picture of you without your shirt on? Just one, please!"

I couldn't say no to her. I took my T-shirt off, turned on the light, clicked a picture, and sent it to her.

"Sorry, I... I got lost in the picture. Abhi, you asked me how could someone be so perfect. Believe me, I ask myself the same question every single time I look at a picture of yours. Sleep well, and I hope you have the best birthday ever."

"I will, now that you're a part of my life..."

The bond between Lieshaa and me kept getting stronger with each passing day. By this point, her father's condition had severely deteriorated and she used to spend most of her time tending to him in the hospital.

One day, she asked me if I ever missed my ex-girlfriend. I straight up told her that I don't talk to other girls, and don't miss my ex.

"Abhi, there's something else... but I'm too scared to ask. But I'll ask anyway. Did you... did you two ever...?"

"Liesh... I can't lie to you. But what we did is now in the past. I'm all yours now."

"Shhh... not another word, please. I got it. I need to be alone for a while... I can't hold back my tears."

I immediately regretted telling her the truth. She was too possessive of me and couldn't bear the idea of me being with someone else, even if it was in the past.

"Abhi, listen. Promise you won't leave me. I'm a simple girl who has a fragile heart. Please don't ever do that with me. My heart won't be able to bear the pain of losing you."

"I swear on my mom, Liesh. I swear on you. Don't ever utter such words again, please. Not even a month ago, we were far apart. Now, we're like a couple of km away from each other."

"But you're still not beside me, Abhi," she replied.

"Soon," I mumbled in my breath.

Now that I look back at her messages and calls, I realize that it was always her who felt that I would leave, and never me. I had never trusted a person to this extent and knew that she would never leave me. She seemed too pure-hearted and innocent to ever think of doing that to me.

I sometimes can't help but laugh at myself while reminiscing about our talks from years ago. She was cheating on her husband with me, but I was sure that she wouldn't do the same to me. A person loses the ability to apply logic when they're in love. They ignore every single red flag, no matter how obvious it is.

I then told her that I was working on a novel based on my short stint in the bank. She got excited and said that she couldn't wait to read it.

"Will you ever write something about me?" she jokingly asked. It's quite ironic that all these years later, here I am, writing a full-fledged novel based on her lies.

When Time Stood Still

A new year had begun. Lieshaa and I were inseparable at this point. Not a day used to pass by without us talking to each other. Staying awake till 3 a.m. just to talk to her had become a daily occurrence for me.

January 4, 2019.

After talking for months on end, Lieshaa and I were about to meet for the very first time. The last time I had seen her up close was behind my college, in 2013. She had spent the past two months or so making daily hospital visits to her father. Her brother was now tending to their father, and she finally managed to take some time out to meet me.

We had agreed to meet at a place about three km from my home. As soon as I reached the spot, I immediately noticed someone getting out of a cab a few feet away from me. It was her! My excitement was at its peak. I was about to meet Lieshaa, the woman of my dreams!

She approached me slowly. Visibly nervous and shy, she was taking her merry time coming towards me, before finally stopping right beside the bike. She smiled at me, and I smiled back at her.

She stood 5'6" tall, a mere four inches short of me. Her straight, long, black hair was flowing to the left, courtesy of gentle gusts of wind. A few strands of her hair were repeatedly coming on her eyes, making her look all the more beautiful. She was wearing a black top, coupled with dark blue jeans. A streetlight stood just beside her, throwing a ray of light on the side of her face, enhancing its glow. Her brown eyes were glistening in all their glory in the dark of the night, and I couldn't help but stare at them without batting an eyelid.

"Liesh, it's been a while... five years to be specific," I said, and we both chuckled before I signaled at her to sit behind me. I started the bike and asked her where should we go.

"As long as I'm with you, I don't care... take me anywhere you wish," she said while grabbing me by the waist and giving me a warm embrace.

Right in front of me was a left turn. On the right, was a building that housed multiple hospitals.

Little did I know that Lieshaa was going to send me to one of these hospitals, sometime in the future.

I quickly turned the bike at the corner and thus kicked off our first ride together. As we were cruising on a flyover, she held me as tightly as she could, and uttered the following words:

"Abhi, I love you."

I was used to hearing those words every day, but the fact that she whispered them in my ears while holding me made it all the more special.

I slowed down the bike and looked behind for a moment. She was staring at me with her beautiful, dreamy eyes, her chin gently placed on my shoulder. At this point, I couldn't resist my urges, and it was evident that she couldn't either.

I stopped the bike shortly after we reached Walker's Street, my favorite place in the city. We then sat close to each other on the pavement, right beside the bike. Lieshaa and I kept staring into each other's eyes while holding hands. It was time.

I slowly leaned in, closed my eyes, and pressed my lips against hers. She grabbed my hair with her right hand while caressing my cheek with her left hand.

We kissed for what seemed like an eternity. It felt like our lips were meant to be locked forever in an endless, perfect kiss. While I was kissing her, I realized that I had never felt such strong emotions for anyone else I had ever been with. At that moment, I was the happiest I had ever been. I was kissing the woman without whom I couldn't imagine a life. If I had died the day after, I would have had zero regrets.

I slowly pulled my lips away from hers and looked directly into her shiny, gemlike eyes. I saw nothing but eternal love for me in those eyes of hers. I hugged her, placed my lips on one of her ears, and whispered, "I'll never stop loving you, Liesh."

That night, I received a string of lengthy messages from her. I still couldn't get her out of my mind and our first kiss was playing on a loop in front of my eyes.

"Abhi, that kiss... I wish time stood still at that very moment. I wish I could be with you all the time. As your wife... forever. I truly feel like you're my husband now. You're everything to me. I love sharing every tiny bit of my life with you. I never wasted my time talking to guys. But with you, no matter how much we talk, it doesn't feel enough.

"There's no one on this earth who can love you the way I do. No matter how shitty my day is, a quick talk with you always makes things right. I love you with all my heart and will continue to do so for the rest of my life, Abhi. I'll go anywhere with you, no questions asked. Rahul had a pic of him and you on his phone. After you left the city, I used to look at it every single day, wondering if you were doing okay. I used to write our names together on blank pages... Lieshaa and Abhilash. I used to look at those two words and realized that they sounded so similar.

"I love you. A LOT. Your nature... I can utter the words "I love you" a thousand times and it still won't be enough. I have feelings for you that I don't have for anyone else, not even Rahul. It's true. I can never lie to you. I'd fallen in love with you the very first time I saw you in your college, without even having talked to you. After you left to pursue an MBA, I used to think about you every single day. Were you happy with your life? Did you have a girlfriend? Did you drink? I used to spend hours thinking about these things. I had zero answers, but I still fell in love with you. Now that I've known you for a while, I know that I fell in love with the right person. The only regret I'll ever have is that we aren't together even though I'm yours. But I promise you, I swear on my mom, I'll always love you. Our love will never die."

The next day, I patiently waited for her call. I couldn't wait to respond to her message. She called at around 11 p.m. I picked it up immediately.

"Liesh... will you marry me?"

"Wha--"

"I'm not kidding in the least. All I'm asking is a year. Let me get a job in the city itself. I'll make some money, save some of it, and we can get married immediately. I'll take you someplace far away from here, just like you want. I'm not mincing my words and have never been this serious about anything. Now, say yes or no, absolutely nothing else."

My proposal was followed by stunned silence from her end. It lasted a couple of seconds and she then responded.

"Yes. A million times yes!"

A week after we met for the first time, Lieshaa's father passed away from cancer. She was inconsolable. The poor woman had now lost both of her parents to cancer. It took quite some time for her to come to terms with her father's death. She needed me more than ever and I always made it a point to prioritize her call over everything else.

On February 20, 2019, I finally bagged a job. I was now a writer working for a sports news website. The pay was good and all I had in mind was to save loads of money over the next year or so and take her away from the city for good.

What the two of us had planned to do was, simply put, evil. But I didn't care.

Lieshaa's plea to take her somewhere far away used to flash in front of my eyes every day. She had made it clear to me that her life had become a living hell and I felt that I was going to be the one to "rescue" her. All I could think of was spending the rest of my life with the woman who had already accepted me as her husband and had promised me eternal love.

Lieshaa and Rahul used to share a phone. Sometime in the summer of 2019, Rahul visited me as he wanted some animated movies for his daughter. I quickly downloaded a bunch and put them on his pen drive.

Rahul also showed me a gym app that he was using for his workouts. I had tried several gym apps in the past, including the one that was on his phone. I still took his phone and pretended to check the app out. Rahul began talking to my brother.

Was I suspicious of Lieshaa? I loved her with every fiber of my being. But when I got hold of the phone, I just couldn't resist checking it out. I didn't find anything on Facebook Messenger, and neither on WhatsApp.

And then I opened the Notepad app.

A single note was saved in it. It had been saved on February 26, 2019. It was quite a long message clearly written by a guy, who was pleading with the receiver (it had to be Lieshaa) to give him a chance. He wrote that he didn't care about physical intimacy and that it was secondary to him, and all he wanted was to be in her presence.

Lieshaa had received a message from a guy and deemed it important enough to save it in the Notes app. I was devastated.

The next time Lieshaa called me, I told her everything. I explained to her that I had found the message that she had saved on her phone and had read it. She didn't say a word for the next few seconds.

And then she began crying.

"I only talk to you, I must've told you a million times that you're the only person I love, and yet you are suspecting me," she said, sobbing.

"I don't want a fight, Liesh. Just tell me who sent that message? It didn't appear magically in that app, did it?" I asked calmly.

"I have no idea, Abhilash. I swear on my mom! Please, believe me. I have never touched a guy, except Rahul and you. NO ONE ELSE. How could...? I beg you... if you can't trust me, this relationship won't last."

I knew that she was lying. But there was absolutely nothing that I could do. I was too much in love at this point to just let her slip away from my hands.

"I believe you, Liesh. More than anyone," I replied.

I knew I couldn't trust her. But my love for Lieshaa had grown to an extent where I couldn't end things with her. She had become everything to me. All I could do was hope that getting caught would teach her a lesson and that it wouldn't happen again.

I can't believe how naive I was.

17 Years in the Making

January 23, 2020.

I grabbed my bike's keys and stormed out of the house. It was 11:30 in the morning. Lieshaa and I had planned to meet at my home for the first time. I started the bike and sped away, wanting to see her as soon as I could.

I picked her up a couple of blocks away from her home. She was wearing black jeans and a pink top, covered with a blue denim jacket. She was also carrying a tiny bag. It was quite chilly out there. She didn't speak a word. We had a fight two days ago and had decided to sort it out at my home. My family was out on vacation.

Lieshaa had been here in 2013. Seven years ago, she stood a few homes away while Rahul picked up a few books for her at my home. As soon as she saw my home, a smile formed on her face.

It had been almost a decade.

I signaled at her to look in the distance. There it was, the home before which Lieshaa once stood, hoping to catch a glimpse of me. Seven long years later, we were both here. Together. In love. We didn't talk to each other even once back then. Now, we were inseparable.

Lieshaa and I entered the house and headed to my room on the terrace. She had suspected that I had been talking to someone else, which I wasn't. I had prepared a detailed speech, explaining that the only calls I got were from her and the folks over at my job. I wanted to look into her eyes and make her believe that I would never cheat on her or betray her trust.

As soon as we entered my room on the terrace, Lieshaa went inside the washroom. I leaned on the door on the other side of the room, waiting for her to come out.

When she came out, I gasped in astonishment. She had changed her clothes and was now wearing a black & white striped one-piece dress. It fitted her to a T and was a thigh-length outfit, which meant that her slender, pretty, insanely long legs were on full display.

She was the prettiest woman I'd ever laid my eyes on. There was not an iota of doubt in my mind at that exact moment that I was going to take her away from this city and marry her.

I approached her, intending to clear things up and end our fight. That didn't happen, though.

Lieshaa quickly put her hands around my shoulders and jumped on me, locking her legs over my body. The hug took me by surprise, but I wasn't complaining one bit. I embraced her with all my might and could feel every bit of her lean, immaculate body.

She then put her feet back on the ground, and without even uttering a single word, planted a kiss on my lips. At this point, neither of us was in the mood to discuss our fight. I carried her toward a corner of the room, gently pushed her against a wall, and pressed my body against hers. I then held her face with both of my hands and brought my lips near hers, making sure that they didn't touch. For the next few seconds, the two of us kept looking at each other, feeling every bit of each other's warm breaths.

"Look at me," I asked her, and she opened her eyes slowly in response. The very next second, I put my lips on hers and began kissing her intensely, while she was still pinned against the wall. She put her hands on my head and grabbed my face as hard as she could while kissing me aggressively.

We were in each other's arms for a couple of hours. Calling it the best two hours of my life would be a massive understatement. I loved her to death. I couldn't bear the pain of ever losing her. I knew that we were meant to be with each other, forever.

We were bound to be together, soon.

About an hour after I dropped her near her home, she called me. We spent the next few minutes talking about how we were all over each other just an hour ago. She then said the following:

"One more thing. Your home is soooooooooooooo beautiful."

"Liesh... please. It's 'our home,'" I corrected her. "Repeat it for me."

"Abhi... you... I can't believe you would say that. I can't tell you how happy that made me."

"Liesh, quickly..."

"Our home!" She responded, a tear running down her cheek.

It was a Sunday evening in early February. I messaged Rahul and asked if he was home. Upon confirming, I picked up the car keys and drove to his home. He had already sent me the map. His home was not more than two km away.

Lieshaa had been living a mere two km away from my home for five long years, hoping that I would see her number in my book and call her.

As I was nearing Rahul's home, I recalled how he sometimes used to visit me to pick me up on his bike, and we would then go to check the project status at the workshop. I vividly remember how once we had to complete our mini-project journal in a hurry and I asked if we could do it at his home. Rahul insisted on doing it at my home, explaining that his place was a tiny room on the terrace.

That day, seven years ago, I could've seen Lieshaa right away if Rahul had agreed to complete the journals at his place. Well, I had to wait for what seemed like ages, but I was now moments away from seeing the place where the love of my life had lived all these years.

His home was now just 500 m away.

I passed by the apartment where we lived for about four years after moving to the city in 1996. I then passed a square and a minute later, I was finally outside his home.

It was a yellow, tiny, two-story building with an attached room on the terrace. I wasn't focused on his home, though.

A big realization had hit me with full force.

I was familiar with this place.

I used to come here all the time, years ago.

But this wasn't the time to go into deep thought. I quickly exited the car and climbed the stairs, finally reaching the terrace. It was quite a large terrace, accompanied by a pretty small room. There was an attached kitchen in the corner of the room, where I could see Lieshaa, probably preparing something for me.

Rahul and I spent a few minutes talking in a corner of the terrace before she called us inside. Rahul's now five-year-old daughter was too busy playing with her toys to even notice me.

"Hi, Abhilash," said Lieshaa, with a big smile on her face, while entering the room. She then handed me a plate of vegetable noodles that she had just made. Rahul then went inside and brought three more plates. He placed one in front of his kid, handed one over to Liesh, and took one for himself.

After I left, I somehow managed to contain my excitement for the next few hours and waited for her call.

"I've been to that place loads of times over the years, Liesh! Let me explain!" I exclaimed, as soon as I picked up her call.

"So, me and my family... we moved from my birthplace to the city in 1996. There's a tiny apartment on the other side of the square that's right outside your colony. We shifted on the second floor and lived there for the next four years, before moving into our own home in 2001.

"My parents put me in a school named Tiny Tots. It's been a while since it closed down. There was a kid who used to live on this very block. I vividly remember that the school bus used to pick him up from this block."

"So, that means... there's a chance you came across me, and possibly Rahul, tens, if not hundreds of times, back in the late 90s! Woah!" Lieshaa was dumbstruck by the coincidence.

"But wait, there's more!" I continued. "In 2005, I failed two straight unit exams in school and my father contacted a teacher who used to take private tuition. There's a large, empty hall at the very end of this block. My brother and I used to go there in a rickshaw for private coaching."

I could picture her eyes widening.

"That's like a couple of houses away from my home, Abhi!" Lieshaa exclaimed.

Lieshaa and Rahul grew up in the same locality. He first saw her sometime in 2006 and began pursuing her. It took about two years, but she ended up accepting his proposal. The duo got married in 2012, about a few months after I first met Rahul in college.

"WHAT????" I was short of words. The realization hit me hard. I couldn't wrap my head around the fact that a young Lieshaa once stood just a few steps away from the place where I spent months on end studying. It made me wonder... did the two of us ever pass by each other back then, at least once?

I will never know, but nothing warms my heart more than the idea that my 14-year-old self once came across a 13-year-old Lieshaa outside that hall.

"Liesh... what the hell? And I'm still not done! As soon as one passes by the hall and turns left, they can see a chain of tiny apartments. In 2008-09, I attended another private coaching class with three other students in one of those apartments, during 12th grade."

"You kept coming back here, Abhi. It's like some divine power wanted you and me to meet." Lieshaa said. "But Rahul once told me that you failed your 12th boards. I couldn't believe it at all and thought that he was joking. Did you really fail, Abhi?" Liesh asked.

"I actually did, Liesh. Long story short: I made the stupidest mistake ever. I attended about two weeks' worth of classes in 11th grade. I used to spend my days playing cricket and visiting video game parlors. The college officials still promoted me to 12th grade by passing me with grace marks. I scored exactly 35/100.

"I repeated the same schtick in 12th class as well. I was so naïve that I didn't even attend the final practical and viva that carried 20 marks for each subject. I somehow managed to survive every subject but failed in maths. I scored 19/100 in maths. If only I had attended the practical and signed the attendance sheets, I would have crossed the passing boundary and a whole year wouldn't have been wasted. Unlike 11th grade, the college couldn't save me this time around.

"On May 31, 2009, I scored 81 in AIEEE. It was enough to get into a good engineering college. I was on cloud nine, Liesh. Four days later, I received my 12th-grade report card. I had failed. It was hands down the worst day of my life. For the next several months, I didn't go out of the house. Didn't meet a single friend. I finally cleared maths during the winter exams.

"Liesh, now that I look back at it, I can't help but feel like it was the best thing that ever happened to me. It sparked a fire in me and I made sure that I would never fail a subject again. But more importantly, a year later, I began pursuing engineering and met Rahul. If I hadn't failed, I would have bagged a way better college based on my score in AIEEE. but fate had other plans, Liesh..."

"Abhi... this doesn't surprise me in the least, to be honest," she said, leaving me confused.

"I didn't get it, Lieshaa," I replied.

"You almost came across me in the late 90s, in the mid-2000s, and then in the late 2000s. Who knows, we even might have passed by each other back then and had no idea we were going to become one someday. Something, maybe destiny, wanted us to meet.

"But it failed. It failed once, twice, and then thrice. And then it got tired of failing. It then designed a situation where you would fail, and get admitted to the SAME college that Rahul was in. I mean, what are the chances, Abhi? And then, we finally met. I saw you in 2013, and you were in my mind and my heart for the next five years, before I finally met you again.

"Abhilash, we were destined to meet someday, and we did. We are destined to be together forever, and we will," a teary-eyed Lieshaa said.

"Yeah Liesh, we will. I can't imagine my life with anyone else but you."

It was finally going to happen. Lieshaa and I had been wanting to turn our dream into reality for quite some time now.

The two of us were meant to be together. We were destined to get married, have children, and spend the rest of our lives raising our happy little family.

I had planned to propose to her in a month or so. I had saved enough money at that point to start afresh with her, somewhere far away. We were going to leave the city and never come back.

There was absolutely nothing that could come between us.

The Great Pause

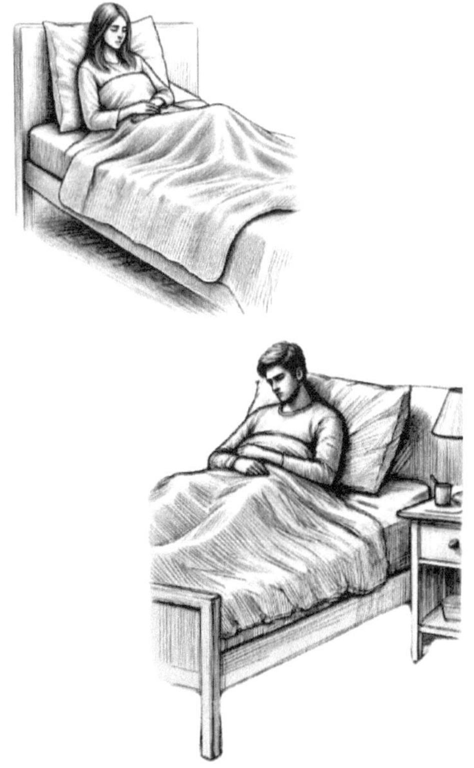

March 11, 2020.

The World Health Organization had declared COVID-19 a pandemic.

I had been hearing and reading about the virus since December as my job as a sports writer demanded active social media usage. With each passing month, the number of COVID-related posts on my Reddit feed kept increasing. And now, it had become a global emergency.

COVID put the entire planet on pause, killed millions of people, put many out of work, and forced everyone to lock themselves inside their homes.

Lieshaa and I had been madly in love with each other for the past two years. She wanted nothing but for me to take her away, marry her, and stay with her till the very end. Although I rejected her proposal at first, I eventually realized that she was the one I wanted to spend the rest of my life with.

I had planned to finally propose to her sometime in March, and then run away with her somewhere far from the city, away from Rahul. On March 11, my plans went down the drain. Two weeks later, a nationwide lockdown was imposed.

Rahul was now working from home. Thus, it became incredibly hard for Lieshaa and me to talk with each other. I had gifted her a small phone not long ago so that she could talk with me without using Rahul's phone. With Rahul now at home at all times, the phone wasn't of much use.

On March 22, the two of us had one of our usual talks. I hadn't told her that I had been planning to propose to her before COVID-19 hit.

After that talk, Lieshaa's calls and messages stopped all of a sudden. She was helpless. A couple of friends of mine had returned home just before the curfew was ordered. My schedule during the pandemic was basically waking up, writing news, binge-watching shows all day, taking random occasional naps, and then spending several hours with my friends at night.

We used to walk for about an hour, play cricket while watching out for police cars, and then sit and talk until 2 a.m. before finally calling it a night. This had become a daily occurrence now. Lieshaa was still in my mind, though. When I didn't receive a call from her for a whole month, frustration kicked in.

I couldn't call or message her in fear of Rahul being at the wrong place at the wrong time and finding out about our affair. All I could do was wait for her to call me, and the fact that she hadn't called me in more than a month was pissing me off.

May 11, 8:12 a.m.

"I miss you." She had FINALLY messaged me. "Rahul is home all the time."

"WHO THE HELL ARE YOU?" I wrote, unable to control my anger.

"Abhilash! You have no idea how much I have been trying to call you for the past few weeks. I'm so angry at you. You've changed. I'll never talk to you again... you're not understanding. Bye forever."

"You've changed," she wrote.

"The irony in your statement," I murmured to myself while reading that message of hers in 2024, four years later.

Lieshaa seldom called or messaged me for the rest of the year. By late 2020, more of my friends had come back to the city to work from home. The curfew was lifted a while ago. Me and my friends began spending a lot of time roaming around the city, partying, and watching movies. It had been about seven months since I had a haircut. I was sporting a massive beard as well. I didn't feel like making myself look presentable. The one for whom I always tried to look good hadn't talked to me in months.

On my 29th birthday, I published *The Rural Banker*, a novel chronicling my short-lived run as a banker in a village, back in 2018. I received congratulatory messages and well-wishes from lots of folks, including Rahul. I was fully expecting to receive a text or a call from Lieshaa, but it never came. The idea that she didn't give a crap about me becoming an author broke my heart. I recalled how she used to get excited over the tiniest of information I shared with her, back when she first contacted me. If my novel had been published back then, she certainly would've poured her heart out while telling me how incredibly proud of me she was.

Now? Not even a text congratulating me.

"I want to know everything about you, Abhi. Your likes, dislikes, your hobbies, what makes you happy, everything. Everything that involves you matters to me. I've spent five years thinking about you. Now that we've finally met, I want to know every little thing about you, no matter how insignificant it is." she once said.

Some people lose interest in you with time. I couldn't fathom the idea that Lieshaa was that person. But the grim reality was impossible to ignore. She certainly wasn't as interested in me now as she was back then.

Around the same time, Rahul caught a severe neck infection and had to be admitted to a hospital. He underwent neck surgery and stayed in the hospital for about a month. Lieshaa called me regularly for the better part of the month since Rahul wasn't around. I knew that it wasn't going to last long though, and it didn't. Rahul was finally discharged and he made a full recovery.

But the worst hadn't come for him yet.

In early to mid-2021, the second wave of COVID-19 struck India, and this surge was way worse and deadlier than the first one.

Rahul lost both of his parents in a span of two weeks. Both of them had succumbed to COVID.

April 20, 2021.

Rahul called me in the morning while I was working and informed me that Lieshaa had caught the virus. She had lost her sense of taste and smell and was now bedridden. I was terrified. I had been dreading this moment and praying it would never come. Unfortunately, it did.

That night, Lieshaa called me.

"Liesh, I... how did this happen? You didn't step outside, did you?"

"Abhi, I'm bedridden. I'm weak as hell. I can't taste, can't smell anything. I'm afraid Abhi..."

"It's all gonna be okay Liesh, trust me. Please take care of yourself."

"Rahul's dad had it. He used to go out without a mask all the time. I didn't say anything, I was scared of saying anything to Rahul. After he caught it, I went downstairs to tend to him on multiple occasions. I wasn't feeling well for the past 4-5 days. Last night, my report arrived. I was positive. I caught it from him, Abhi. He's no more, and I think I'm go--"

"Shhh! Liesh, not another word. I beg you. This can't happen. This won't happen. Such a healthy, young woman... full of energy... you will get well soon Liesh. I promise you," I tried to do my best to assure her that nothing was going to happen to her. But deep down inside, I was scared for her life.

"I'm living alone in the terrace room for the next 10 days or so, Abhi. You can call me anytime you want. I'm probably not going to last long anyway. I wanna talk to you as much as I can..."

"Can you stop being negative, Liesh? It will only worsen your health. Please. You need to relax and take your mind off it. Please, for me."

"Abhi, I will get well soon, right? I'm scared."

"You will, I swear to God," I said, wiping tears off my face.

"Can you... I'm not in a condition to even look at the phone screen for long. Abhi, I have a request. Can you tell me about all the necessary measures one needs to take once they've tested positive?"

I spent the next several hours researching on the web and jotted down a list of things one needed to do if they caught the virus. Keeping yourself hydrated, drinking lots of fluids, following the doctor's instructions to the T, and taking lots of rest were just a few of several points that I had noted, before sending her the list.

"Liesh, I offered Rahul monetary help when he called today but he told me that he had enough money for the time being. Listen to me very carefully. If there's a need, don't hesitate one bit to ask for money. I'm ready to empty my bank account, but you need to get better. And don't argue with me on this, please. JUST ASK. I'm here for you."

"Thanks, my love. I don't know why this happened to me, but I feel so lucky that you're trying to do so much for me. I love you. And trust me, I will ask you if there's a need for money. Who else would I ask?"

A week later, Lieshaa got tested again. This time around, the report was negative. I breathed a sigh of relief. I couldn't fathom the idea of a world without Lieshaa in it.

On May 6, I caught a fever. I was back to normal again in three days but then realized that I couldn't smell anything. The sense of taste was still there, though. On May 10, I tested positive for COVID. The next day, she messaged me.

"Shit! You're positive! How did... Abhi, you told me you never step foot outside the house. Rahul told me this morning that you caught it."

"I must've caught it from a food delivery guy. We did order a lot of food during the second wave."

"Abhi, drink lots of water. And don't reduce your food intake. Stay in your room for the next 20 days. We're young, you'll soon get better, just like I did. Please take care of yourself. Eat boiled eggs and don't spend too much time on your phone. And sleep as much as you can. I'm sure you will get better in a few days."

Thankfully, Lieshaa was right. 10 days after I tested positive, I got tested again. This one came negative. I still spent a few more days in quarantine, though, just to be safe.

The pandemic had slowly died down by late 2021. Lieshaa and I both survived the pandemic, but it seemed like it had strained our relationship. Lieshaa and Rahul had now shifted downstairs where Rahul's parents used to live. They spent the remainder of the year getting the ground floor renovated.

In the past, Rahul had asked me for monetary help on a couple of occasions and I never said no to him. Now? He owned three flats, a farm, and a lot of money that he had inherited from his parents. He was filthy rich now, and so was she.

October was here, and Lieshaa hadn't talked to me since I recovered from COVID. Did she grow close to Rahul during the pandemic? Had she gotten bored of me? I couldn't begin to imagine a scenario where she wasn't interested in me. Now that the pandemic had died down, I wanted to finally go ahead with what I had planned for her and myself.

But was she still down for it?

The Dilemma

Someone who couldn't live a day without talking to you, now goes months on end without saying a word.

How would that make you feel?

On October 11, I decided to call Lieshaa. It was a massive risk as Rahul could end up receiving the call, but I had had enough at this point.

"HOW DO YOU LOOK IN THE MIRROR EVERY DAY?" I screamed at her as soon as she picked up the phone. My fingers were trembling.

"Rahul is right in front of me all the time... Abhi. I tried, I really did. But I just couldn't call," she replied.

"You couldn't call, or am I used goods now? Did you find someone else? If you let me know, I'll stop bothering you right away, Lieshaa."

"How dare you?" She asked. "You have no idea what I go through every day... I've told you repeatedly that you're the only one that I love with all my heart... and this is what you have to say? Abhi... there's a sanitizer right in front of me. I'll dri--"

"SHUT THE HELL UP!" I couldn't take it anymore. This wasn't the first time that she had teased harming herself. "Five months! FIVE MONTHS, you liar! You claim to love me, yet you manage to go five freaking months without contacting me even once?

"I'm not here to fight. All I'm saying is that I have wasted enough time. It seems like you feel I don't have anyone else except you," I said. "I want you to know that someone has been pursuing me for some time now. And judging by this demeanor of yours, I would be better off being with her. You take care, Liesh."

"What... you... GO TO HELL! You do that, Abhi. Go meet whoever is out there, waiting for you. Go sleep with her, marry her, and never call me again," she yelled, before hanging up.

I figured it was all over between us. The next evening, she called me.

"Listen. In sorry. I love you... I haven't slept in the last 24 hours. Can you visit us tonight? I will prepare Butter Chicken and I want you to taste it. Just call Rahul and tell him you want to visit."

"ABSOLUTELY NOT! You want me to come, and all I get is to see you and realize that you're not mine? The urge to grab you by the arms and kiss you repeatedly... I won't be able to sit there and just look at you, knowing you aren't mine anymore."

"I AM YOURS! FOREVER, ABHILASH! Okay, let's meet at your home soon. But please don't meet anyone else. I'm begging you," she pleaded.

"Are you serious?"

"I swear on you, Abhilash. I'm a simple girl, I've never hurt anyone. I can't even talk to guys without feeling uneasy. But with you, it's different. I have a question, though... please, don't lie. Is... is she better than me? I mean not in terms of looks, but her nature... I need to know."

"Liesh... she's a good person, but you gotta understand. If I felt that she was better than you, I would not have called you all of a sudden five months later. I would've started dating her without letting you know. You managed to go five months without saying a word and I felt that you didn't even deserve a call after what you did. But I'm too much into you, and wanted to try at least once before moving on."

"Rahul... he's in front of me all the time. I wish I could... but we'll meet and talk. Believe me, please. And don't talk to her, whoever she is. It's a request."

"I promise! But Liesh, can you promise me something as well?"

"Yeah. Anything. Whatever you want. I'm serious."

"Promise me... that you'll always love me. And you'll never leave me. I've realized over the years that I won't be able to live if you ever leave me."

"Never. NEVER. I promise you. We complete each other, Abhilash. That's why God finally brought us together after trying for years on end," she assured me.

Rahul called me a few days later. It was his daughter's sixth birthday. That night, I bought a large chocolate box and headed to his house.

Rahul and Lieshaa now lived downstairs. The entire first floor had been renovated. The dining room was brightly lit, had a large TV mounted on a wall, had a big couch on a side, and looked like a lot of money had gone into renovating it.

While Rahul was showing me the renovated rooms, I suddenly heard her voice. I turned and saw her coming out of the kitchen. Draped in a dark green saree, she smiled at me and nodded.

She stood right under those shiny, bright lights, making the gold necklace on her milky-white neck sparkle.

She had never looked prettier.

"Abhilash, it's been ages since you last visited us," she exclaimed.

It was a small party. Rahul hadn't called anyone else except me and a few kids from his daughter's class. He was keen on showing me the newly renovated home. After the cake was cut, I decided to take my leave.

Rahul brought a selfie stick from the bedroom, wanting to click some photos.

He secured his phone on the selfie stick holder and signaled to me to sit on the couch at the extreme left. He then sat beside me, putting his daughter on his lap. A hesitant Lieshaa stood at the bedroom door, watching us. Rahul called her and her eyes beamed with joy. She quickly sat beside him.

Suddenly, I felt something behind me. She had extended her hand past Rahul's back, placing it gently on mine.

The smile on my face while posing for the picture couldn't have been more genuine.

I visited them the next day as well. Rahul had informed me that he was holding a *sraddha* in remembrance of his late parents. I parked my car beside an empty plot as the road in front of his home was covered with a pandal (tent). Lieshaa was serving food to an old couple. She was wearing a white saree and had no makeup on. It didn't stop her from looking drop-dead gorgeous, though.

Rahul brought me inside. This was the first and the last time that I met Lieshaa's grandmother and brother. He seemed likable and quite easy to talk to, and so was Lieshaa's grandma. Rahul then asked me if I wanted to eat.

I then took a plate, filled it with food, and began eating in a corner. Rahul quickly put up two chairs beside me. I took a chair, while he sat on the other one. Rahul suddenly noticed that a few more guests had arrived and quickly made a call to Lieshaa, who was inside the house.

"Can you please come outside quickly? More guests have arrived while you're busy inside," he was angry at her. Maybe it was the stress of arranging such a large ceremony.

"I would never treat her that way," I thought to myself.

I saw Lieshaa storming out of the home and attending to the guests. After she was done with them, she took a chair, placed it in front of us, and took her seat. The three of us chatted for a while as I finished my food.

Rahul then sent me the pictures that he had clicked the night before. The ones in which she had placed her hand on my back. They had now become prized possessions for me. Lieshaa had her eyes glued on me as Rahul walked with me to the car. I waved at him and stole a glance at her while reversing the car, before driving away.

"Do something, anything... but please don't go," Lieshaa was an emotional wreck and couldn't stop crying. I hugged her and began caressing her back gently. We were sitting beside each other in my room. Downstairs, my brother was asleep in his room. My parents weren't home.

It had been about a month since my back-to-back visits to Lieshaa's home. In the third week of November, I received an offer for a job that came with insanely good pay. The job location was Pune, the same city that took me away from her seven years ago. I informed Lieshaa about the offer that very night.

Mere two days later, I received a call from her in the morning.

"12:30, in front of my college," she hurriedly said, before cutting the call. I picked her up from the college she used to attend back in the day.

We pounced on each other as soon as we entered my room. Minutes later, I grabbed her by the hand and took her to the bathroom. We stood right under the shower head, staring into each other's eyes before I turned it on.

The warm water cascaded over the two of us, slowly dripping down our faces while we passionately kissed each other's wet lips. It didn't take long before both of us were completely drenched in water. We couldn't keep our hands off each other for the next hour or so.

After coming out, I took a towel and asked her to dry herself. As she was about to take the towel, I pulled it away from her and grabbed her by the waist, bringing her closer to me.

"Keep still," I told her, and kept rubbing the towel gently against her hair until it was completely dry. I then started wiping her face and worked my way down to her feet.

A few minutes later, we were comfortably seated beside each other on the side of my bed. She told me to consider not leaving.

"This is my worst nightmare, Abhi. It's like history is about to repeat itself. You left years ago, and while Rahul was bidding you goodbye, I was at home, crying my heart out.

"Now, you want to leave me again. You know very well you and I both won't be able to live without each other. And if you've already made up your mind, I want you to look into my eyes and tell me that you're leaving me again," she said, her eyes having turned red due to incessant crying.

"Hey, hey," I brought her closer to me and gave her a peck on the cheek. After being on the fence for the past several hours, I had finally made a decision.

A few days later, Rahul's family and I went to the mall for bowling and pizza. I wanted to give her a treat after choosing to stay. I told Rahul that I had a game card that was about to expire and was wondering if he would like to come along for a game of bowling.

I reached the mall 20 minutes before their arrival, bought a game card, and recharged it as well. A pizza party followed and I had a tough time keeping my eyes off her in front of him. As Rahul, Lieshaa, and their daughter were leaving, Lieshaa looked at me, and we waved each other goodbye.

As the year was nearing its end, Rahul called me and told me that he needed my help. He needed a third party's (witness) signature on an important document that he had applied for. I immediately said yes. I had always been willing to help him. Also, I would get to see Lieshaa again. I could never grow tired of seeing her adorable face.

I reached the administrator's office via a cab and saw them sitting on a bench at the other end. A two-hour wait commenced. Lieshaa soon got bored and took her daughter to the campus garden that was right in front of us. While Rahul talked with the agent that he had hired, I kept looking at her as she played with her daughter.

Lieshaa then put her on a swing and began pushing her gently, her eyes locked with mine. She then saw a toddler approaching her on all fours, while his mom shouted at him from a distance. She quickly picked him up and took him to his mom.

The sight of Lieshaa holding that child sparked something in me. All I could imagine at that moment was Lieshaa holding our child someday.

Perfect for Each Other

January 23, 2022, 11:00 a.m.

"Abhi...

"Yes, Liesh?"

"I have to attend my friend's wedding tonight. Can we meet for an hour or so before I go?"

"Have I ever said no to you? Hell yeah, I'll meet you!"

That night, I picked her up from the far end of her locality. She had makeup on, was carrying a bouquet in her hand, and was draped in a red saree. Her lips were adorned with pink lipstick. A crystal drop earring on each ear was only adding to her unrivaled charm. She looked like she had come straight out of a dream.

That massive saree of hers made it quite hard for her to sit on the pillion seat of my bike. She somehow managed to sit in a side-saddle position, and off we went.

The two of us entered my room and immediately embraced each other. An hour or so passed. She was firmly seated on the side of the bed while I was helping her reapply lipstick. She was going to be late for the wedding.

"I have been wanting to ask you something for quite some time now," I said while putting the lipstick in her purse.

"What is it, Abhi?"

"Liesh, I've known you for almost a decade now. No matter how many times you text me or call me, it never gets tiring. I pick up my phone and respond to you with the same enthusiasm. EVERY. SINGLE. TIME. I know for a fact that I'm never gonna get tired of seeing your pretty, innocent face. Those sparkling eyes of yours... I could stare into them for hours on end and it still wouldn't be enough. Every time I hold your hands, I feel complete. I want this feeling to last forever, Li--"

"Shhh! as I've always said... A MILLION TIMES YES, Abhi!"

I quickly grabbed her and kissed her like there was no tomorrow. I then put my hand on her cheek, caressing it softly.

"Liesh, no need to utter another word. And the same goes for me. I've never been this happy before. This is as perfect as a moment can get. I don't want to say anything that might ruin it. Liesh... I'll love you till my last breath. That's a promise," I said, before putting my lips on hers once again.

The day wasn't far. I knew what I had to do. Lieshaa and I were destined to be together forever. The pure joy on her face when I told her what I had in mind... it was the most beautiful sight my eyes had ever come across.

She called me the next day.

"Abhi, I have something to say… you left me in 2014. I truly believe that God brought you back to me. Now, I don't want to lose you, ever."

"Liesh... just a few days, and we're going to be together. Forever, this time around. Every bit of me is yours. Everything I own is yours. Every single penny I've earned over the past three years is yours. The only reason I wake up and work is to make sure I will have enough when we're together and I can give you anything you ask of me."

"I love you... I love you... I love you... I'll keep saying it, and it still won't be enough, Abhilash. Can you do something for me? Can you run your fingers through my hair while I lie on your lap? I've never told you this, but I've dreamed about it countless times."

"Lieshaa, I will. I can't wait to do that every day for the rest of our lives."

A few days passed. Rahul had called me again. He had bought a new laptop and didn't need my old one anymore. My uncle had been asking me for one for a while. I decided to take my old laptop from Rahul and give it to my uncle.

Rahul and Lieshaa urged me to have dinner with them, but I had to hand over the laptop to my uncle in a hurry. I got out of their house and approached my car.

"Can you give them a quick ride in your car?" Rahul asked, pointing at Lieshaa and his daughter.

"Why not? Hop in!" I said, excitedly.

Lieshaa's daughter sat beside me on the front seat, while she took the back seat. I drove around the area for a couple of minutes. My right hand was firmly holding the steering wheel while the left one was placed on hers.

I dropped them in front of Rahul's home and took off, a big smile forming on my face.

"I was the one who asked Rahul if he could ask you to give us a quick ride. I didn't want you to leave," Lieshaa said that night.

"That's so sweet of you, Liesh... I wish I could've stayed longer."

"Abhi, don't you think we're perfect... I mean, for each other? Like, our height..."

"We are, Liesh! You're almost as tall as me. I'm 5 feet 10, what about you?"

"I'm 5 feet 6, Abhi. I'm slightly taller than Rahul. But when I stand beside you in front of the mirror... I can't help but keep staring. I've come across hundreds of couples, but there's something special about the two of us."

I immediately recalled the two of us clicking mirror selfies at my home that day. Tons of them. Smiling at the mirror, smiling at each other, locking lips, hugging, me holding her in my arms... there wasn't a pose we didn't try.

"Liesh... the fact that I have like a hundred pictures of us together speaks volumes about how much you trust me," I said. "I promise you, I'll never break your trust."

"Abhi, you don't even need to bring it up. I trust you with my eyes closed and my back turned," she responded.

I had countless pictures of us together that we had taken over the years. Every one of them was a prized possession to me. I had also saved every text conversation we had had over the years. Every single one of those thousands of messages, right from the very first one where she asked if I remember her, held a very special place in my heart. There was no way I could delete any of them.

I always made it a point, though, to remind her to erase every conversation of ours to make sure Rahul wouldn't catch us.

Rahul was going to see those pictures and texts of us less than two years from this very moment.

"You'll always be mine, right? If you leave me... Abhi, I simply won't be able to live. We only have one life, and I want to spend it with you. Till the very end. Never change, Abhi, please. When I lost my mom and then my dad, I was numb. I couldn't understand why God was punishing me. I had no idea I would start seeing my mom and dad in you, Abhi," she said.

"Liesh... what are you saying? You... I'll never forget what you just said. I love you. And I need to say something as well. Liesh, I've seen people telling their loved ones that they would give their lives for each other. I never understood that. Why would you even think of giving your life for someone who isn't your blood and family?

"I never got it. Until I met you, Liesh. Now I understand, 'cause I can say the same without a shadow of a doubt... if the time comes, I would give my life for you, I want you to know that."

Deep down inside, I knew that there was not a shred of lie in what I had just said.

"Shhh... don't say that, Abhilash. That day... in your room. The moment you told me you wanted to marry me, I was like, "You... are you serious? This isn't a dream, right?" I had a hard time believing that the guy I love the most wanted me to be his wife, forever. I'm as simple and innocent as they come, Abhi... please don't ever betray me. I have a pure heart that can't even think of hurting anyone. I'll be yours forever, that's a promise."

"Liesh, we'll be spending the rest of our lives in each other's arms. In less than a month, we're going to be together."

"Abhilash, will you... will you really accept me as your wife? Please... please take me away somewhere far away... I need you..."

"Liesh... the day is inching near. I don't like lying to you. Please, believe me. You know, I keep imagining the two of us in the kitchen, cooking stuff and eating together, taking a walk, going shopping, enjoying a drive, and so much more..."

"Really? Abhi, I love how you said we'll cook food together. Rahul never helps me, I hate that so much. But I'm sure you'll keep kissing me instead of cooking anything and we'll end up ordering food, won't we?"

"That seems about right, Liesh!" I chuckled. "You... you'll never leave me, right"?

"Never, Abhi. I swear on my mother's grave. Believe me..."

"I do. And always will! Good night, Lieshaa!"

"One sec, Abhi..."

"Yeah?"

"I love you."

"I love you too, my everything!"

Part III
Lieshaa leaves

Dark

March 14, 2022, 11:19:54 p.m.

"Abhilash..."

"Nothing."

"I love you"

"But..."

"You'll soon find out why I can never meet you again..."

She had sent a string of texts.

"Liesh... WHAT? WHAT HAPPENED? Pick up my call, please! Is this your idea of some sick joke?"

"Please... Rahul is sleeping next to me. Don't call, please," she wrote.

"The stuff you just wrote... are you serious?" I was SHAKING.

"Yeah, Abhi. I am."

"You... you betrayed me. You lied to me. All my hopes... at least tell me the reason why you're ending it all of a sudden before I block you."

"You can, right away," her blunt message stated. That was a clear indicator that she was keen on ending it quickly without much drama. She WANTED me to block her.

"Liesh... we were planning to flee, marry each other, live together till our last breaths. Please, at least tell me what made you change your mind after making promises and stringing me along for four freaking years!"

"Rahul... he is the reason."

"No... Rahul isn't the reason. It's you, Liesh. You are ending this."

"Whatever you wanna believe," her message read.

"I'm blocking you now. I want to say a lot of things, but I have no strength left in me. Remember one thing, though. I'll never... I'll NEVER forget, never forgive what you did. My hopes... your lies... four years... I'll always remember this betrayal. I'll never forget your lies..."

And just like that, my world came crashing down in a matter of seconds. I was scared, confused, and my fingers were trembling in anger while I read her final messages.

Every assurance, every promise of hers, every declaration of love, all of her messages began flashing right before my eyes...

"My dear mom, please make sure Abhilash and I are together forever."

"I love you so much... I can't live without you..."

"Abhi, I love your eyes, your hair, your lips... what I'm trying to say is that you're perfect!"

"I've never loved someone as much as you. Not even Rahul. Believe me."

"I want you to know that I'll love you till my last breath."

"There's no one on this earth who can love you the way I do. I have feelings for you that I don't have for anyone else, not even Rahul."

"Our love will never die."

Countless promises of eternal love... it took her a minute to destroy everything.

I didn't think much about our last conversation for a few days. I was fully expecting her to call me in a week or so, to patch things up between us.

That call never came. And I started panicking.

Everything changed. No matter what I did, be it working, going out with friends, or spending time with family, I couldn't take her out of my mind. I couldn't believe that after years' worth of promises, she had thrown me away like what we had didn't mean anything.

It was unfathomable to me that someone who couldn't go a day without talking to me had suddenly cut all contact. Watching a movie, reading a book, or working out... everything turned into a chore. Why would I watch a movie when there was no call to look forward to after finishing it? Why would I read a damn book, when all I wanted was to read her texts? What was the point of working out when the only reason I was doing it was to look good for her?

Depression was slowly setting in, but this was only the beginning. Things were about to get much, much worse. Back in late 2021, after not hearing from Lieshaa for five straight months, I told her that someone was pursuing me and valued me unlike her. That made Lieshaa plead with me to stop talking to her.

I wasn't lying.

There WAS a girl named Rachna who was into me and had expressed her interest in me on multiple occasions. I ended up rejecting her for Lieshaa, just like I rejected Vani in 2018.

Lieshaa wasn't around anymore. I hadn't lost hope, though. When someone who once promised you the world suddenly leaves, it hurts you in more ways than one. My mental health was quickly deteriorating. When this happens, a person tends to do the craziest, stupidest things.

I did one too. The first of many.

In late April, I messaged Rahul and told him that I had accepted the job offer that I had previously rejected a few months ago, and was leaving for Pune in June.

Then, I messaged Rachna and told her the same, leaving her devastated. I asked her if she wanted to go on a night drive with me. She happily said yes. She was glad I was at least willing to meet her before leaving the city. I bought two sweet boxes and drove to the place where I was supposed to meet her.

"I couldn't believe my eyes when I read your message! I'm so happy we've finally met! How am I looking?" she asked, looking at me with dreamy eyes.

"You look insanely good!" I replied, smiling at her.

She was extremely beautiful. There was no doubt about that. Maybe, just maybe... she was prettier than Lieshaa.

But she wasn't Lieshaa.

I was hoping that her pretty face would work in my favor. What I was about to do was pure evil. I was crossing lines one after the other. But I was too desperate to care.

I handed her a box of sweets and told her that I needed to give the other one to a relative of mine.

We drove to Rahul's home next. I called to inform him that I was coming to hand over a box of sweets. I stopped the car in front of his home. He came out, opened the gate, and approached me.

"Come inside," he cheerfully said, while taking the box. I signaled at Rachna and told him that I had to drop her home by 10.

And then she came out.

Lieshaa was at the door. The woman who had destroyed me from within was staring at me, giving me her characteristic blank look. I made sure to stay and talk to Rahul until she got a good look at Rachna. She kept staring at the two of us, firmly standing at the door. I wish I knew what was going on in her mind.

Now, Rahul would tell her that I was leaving, just like I did in 2014. Also, she had seen me with a much, much more beautiful girl, something that she had always feared. All that was left to do was wait.

I spent the next hour driving around the city with Rachna. She seemed pretty sad that I was leaving and kept telling me how much she liked me. I wasn't budging, though. I was told the same thing by someone else for years before being mercilessly dumped.

Someone who seemed like the most cheerful person when she first messaged me five years ago, and was getting overly excited about every little thing I was sharing with her. There was a stark contrast between that Lieshaa and the one who recently dumped me. Her final message was dry, dismissive, and she didn't put even the tiniest effort into hiding the fact that she didn't care about me anymore.

It had worked! She messaged me the very next day.

"Abhi... why the hell did you bring that girl to my home? What were you trying to do? Were you trying to show off? Were you trying to tell me that you have options if I'm gone?" she immediately brought up what had happened the night before.

I WAS LIVID.

"Yes, I was trying to convey that very message. And yes, you did leave me. YOU ABSOLUTE HYPOCRITE! Remember how you once told me that a guy had somehow gotten your number and was repeatedly bothering you? And when I got worried, you told me that you were just trying to see my reaction!

"Such disgusting and manipulative games are fine and dandy, until someone plays them with you, right?" I furiously asked.

"Sigh... I don't want to argue. We've got a new member in our family... and Abhi, you should've at least told me before deciding to leave. Anyways, best of luck for your future," she wrote, before sending a picture of herself with a tiny, white puppy.

"Oh... so that's it? That's all you've got to say to me? I can't explain how utterly frustrating it is that you've conveniently ignored what you did to me. Now, I'm about to leave and all you have for me is a lousy "best of luck?" Is it that easy for you to forget everything you said? I would love to know how you manage to sleep at night, Liesh."

"Abhi, I'm in pain... I have a fever and I'm bedridden. I'm sorry, I can't even look at the phone for long," she wrote.

"STOP IGNORING MY MESSAGES! Are you even reading what I wrote?" I was fuming. "Okay, can you... can you at least do one thing? I'll send you a message by tomorrow evening. All you need to do is read it and respond to it. I ask nothing else from you. Can you do it?"

"I will, Abhi..." she said, before immediately going offline.

One thing that I noticed was the way she was responding to my messages, and it broke my heart.

When she met me five years ago, I was the most important person in her life. Her eyes used to be fixated on the screen, eagerly waiting for every new message. Responding to my messages used to be her priority, with every other person taking a backseat to me. Every text of mine used to receive a quick response from her. No matter how many messages I sent, she made it a point to respond to every single one.

Now?

Everything had changed. Once a person is done with you and isn't interested in you anymore, it reflects on the way they respond to your messages. She was replying to my messages from the notification panel itself. While I, in desperation, was sending quick replies, she was taking her merry time with every single response. It was evident that I wasn't her priority anymore, and it hurt like hell.

Since she "couldn't" talk on a call, I spent hours upon hours writing a lengthy message. I reminded her of the promises that she had made, our never-ending vows to love each other for an eternity, the way I used to hold her, kiss her, and how safe and secure she always felt around me. I asked her to explain what was the issue, and maybe we could work on it, as I had invested four long years in her and wanted to spend the rest of my life with her as well.

I then came to the point. I asked her if she was really okay with me leaving. Not too long ago, she had pleaded with me not to leave her alone. Once I left, it would be all over. Was she really going to let me go after spending the past four years assuring me that she couldn't live without me?

That night, at around midnight, she finally read the message and responded.

"Please don't go, Abhi. Please. Ok, tell me something... will you be able to live without me?"

"Liesh... you literally said it's over. And that we're never meeting again. I've been through hell for the past several weeks. Only if you could feel what I've been feeling since you ended things..."

"Abhi. I need to tell you something," she replied. "I can't lie to you... for several months now, Rahul and I have been planning to have another kid. I don't know what's happening... I had a miscarriage. Maybe the fact that I had COVID had something to do with it. But we're still trying. We've decided to wait for a few months before trying again.

"I won't force you to stay, Abhilash. I don't want to spoil someone's career and future. If you decide to leave, don't forget me, please," she wrote.

I was numb. I was crying incessantly. I couldn't feel anything at that very moment. It felt as if she had reached down my throat, grabbed my heart, pulled it out, and squished it right in front of me.

Lieshaa. The woman who had promised me she was mine. Wanted to have a child with me. Wanted me to take her away from Rahul and spend the rest of my life with her.

She had been planning to have another kid with her husband while she assured me every single night that she would be mine forever.

A month ago, she was pleading with me to take her somewhere far away. At the same time, she was at home, trying for a baby with her husband. While she was making promises to me, deep down inside, she was thinking of ways to dump me. And she ended up doing it in the bluntest way possible.

"WHA... WHAT? Liesh... a baby?? But you and I... what are you doing?"

I pressed send. A single gray tick appeared at the end of the message.

Not only did she ignore my text asking her why she betrayed me, but she didn't feel like talking to me at all and decided to go offline. It was clear as day that she didn't want to continue the conversation.

I was everything to her not too long ago. Now, I was just another guy who was bothering her to the point that she decided to switch off the internet and go to sleep instead.

I had become a nuisance to the woman I loved with all my heart.

It was 1 a.m. I was alone in the room. The lights were off.

It was pitch dark.

I was lying in a corner of my bed, tears rolling down my face. It felt as if I was going to have a panic attack. I somehow calmed myself down, took a sip of water, and closed my eyes. This was the exact moment I realized I was suffering from depression. There was nothing to look forward to in my life anymore.

To this day, I haven't been able to forget what I went through that night. It was hands down the worst night of my life. That dark, grim, wretched night left me completely broken inside.

Full Circle

The plane had finally landed in Bangalore. I headed outside as soon as I got my suitcase. I intended to take the shuttle bus to the campus as it was way cheaper than booking a cab. My 10-day pre-joining bank training was going to start tomorrow.

As soon as I reached the shuttle bus stop, it started drizzling. Instead of trying to find cover to prevent myself from getting wet, I simply stood there.

I stood there and took it all in.

The beautiful weather of Bangalore. The sky was cloaked in a soft, grayish hue, making for a cozy setting. The air was fresh and I could smell the earthy scent of the wet soil, coming from the nearby garden.

I was out there, more than 1000 km from my hometown. Back there, a beautiful, caring woman was missing me, and was dying to hear from me as soon as possible. She wanted me more than anyone in the world.

At that moment, I didn't know how good I had it. I also didn't have the slightest idea that it wasn't going to last forever.

I quickly got on the bus and took my earphones out. It was a two-hour ride to the training campus.

I suddenly woke up. I was dreaming again.

2018. A new job. Bangalore. Lieshaa's texts EVERY SINGLE NIGHT. She loved me so much. Where did those days go? How did things change so drastically? Why did she leave me when she swore on her mom that she wouldn't?

The room was still dark and gloomy. My face had dried up. My lips were flaky. It seemed as if I hadn't touched a glass of water in ages. My lifeless eyes kept staring at the ceiling for an hour straight before I got up.

I was depressed, but work wasn't going to wait.

I immediately messaged her again. Multiple messages. Long paragraphs. Hoping that she just might change her mind and come back to me. I told her how I couldn't live without her. How I yearned to talk to her, to read her messages, to hear her utter the words, "I love you, Abhi!"

She replied at noon.

"Abhi, I'm not well. I can't even get up from bed. I still love you... A LOT. But what can I do? I'm married... I'm scared... what if he... if I wasn't married, I would've stayed with you for the rest of my life. I have the same feelings for you that you have for me. Again, I only love YOU, but you refuse to understand my problems," her message read.

My eyes couldn't believe what I had just read.

Her hypocrisy was astounding.

My mind wandered back to 2018 when she was trying her best to make me hers. That conversation was now flashing before my eyes...

"Abhilash, I need you to ask you something very important. Do... do you love me?"

"Lieshaa, it's not right and you know that. You're married. To my friend."

"Ok... sorry. But then we shouldn't even talk to each other. That's wrong as well, right?"

"Talking, I feel, is harmless, Lieshaa. But if that bothers you, we can stop it. I've no issues whatsoever, even though it would hurt a little."

"I love you so much... I can't live without you..."

Back in 2018, when I wasn't hers and she professed her love for me, I reminded her that she was my friend's wife.

She didn't care. She wasn't scared. The fact that she was married didn't mean anything to her.

Now, after a four-year affair, it suddenly dawned on her that she was married.

Four years ago, I betrayed my friend's trust and began an affair with his wife. It took a while, but karma had finally caught up to me.

It had been quite some time since my self-respect had gone down the drain. I was repeatedly begging her to talk to me, to try to understand what she was doing to me, and to keep the promises that she had made over the years.

Unfortunately, this was just the beginning.

"Liesh, can I say something? Please promise me, you won't go offline mid-conversation." The next night, I begged her to not leave me hanging like she had been doing lately. How did it all come to this? The woman who considered me her everything was now avoiding me like the plague. "You used to talk to me every single day. I'm not asking that anymore... all I ask of you is to talk to me at least once a week. At least ask me how I'm doing… is it too much to ask?"

She couldn't go a day without talking to me in the beginning. Now, I was desperately pleading with her to talk to me at least once every few days. Looking back now, this was one of the lowest points of my life.

"What's the matter, Abhi?" she wrote. Her casual tone, despite knowing full well what she had done, was incredibly annoying.

"I had a request. If I did something that turned you off, if I made a mistake that made you leave me, please... please tell me so that I can make things right. Please tell me, I'll try to improve myself, but don't leave me. You've left me a broken man, Liesh. All alone, there's nothing left to look forward to," I pleaded.

"No Abhi, you're not at fault. It's just that... I'm not well Abhi. My mind isn't working. I need rest. Two miscarriages have taken a toll on my body."

"Liesh, how did... you were promising me the world, and at the same time, trying for a baby with him. How could you do this to me, Liesh? How could such a sweet and kind soul turn into this... this two-timing..."

"Abhi... believe me, please believe me. I didn't want it, but these people kept pleading with me. Even my grandma kept requesting me to have another kid with him until I finally caved in," she replied.

"But Liesh... you wanted to marry me, you wanted a child with me. Don't you remember?"

"I did, but you said no, Abhi."

"But I did say yes later, and you were the happiest that you had ever been in your life. You wanted me to take you somewhere away from here, Liesh. It can still happen. I can still give you a baby... I want a girl... you've seen us in the mirror, right? Imagine Liesh, we will have the cutest and the most adorable girl ever." I wrote.

She then said something that filled me with hope, once again.

"Whatever it is, it will be ours, Abhi."

A week later, something happened that made me realize that it was truly over. I went to a party with a friend. While having dinner, a piece of bread got stuck in my throat. My friend helplessly watched as I began choking on it and coughing repeatedly. Tears began running down my cheeks. I immediately opened Google Images and typed the term "Heimlich Maneuver" in it, before showing the photos to my friend.

He quickly grabbed me from behind and began performing the move. Thankfully, the piece of bread came out in the second attempt!

After messaging her for two straight days, she finally responded.

"Sorry. Rahul... I couldn't. What happened?" she seemed hasty.

I told her what had happened to me two days ago. How I seemingly escaped death after almost choking on a piece of bread.

"Oh shit! But... but I'm glad you're okay. Wait, I'll message you in a while," she wrote back, and immediately went offline. She didn't message again.

Lieshaa was a massive cricket fan, unlike me. My fandom had died years ago, way back during the 2007 Cricket World Cup. About two months after Lieshaa dumped me, legendary Australian cricketer Andrew Symonds tragically passed away in an accident. Lieshaa had posted a tribute picture on her Instagram handle following his death.

She once told me that the idea of living without me scared her. Now, after I almost dropped dead, all she could come up with was a quick message that made it clear that she couldn't give two shits about my well-being. On the other hand, she shared a heartfelt picture paying tribute to someone she had never met.

I had become a non-entity in her eyes. And it hurt like hell.

I had stopped crying a long time ago. At that moment, I couldn't help but smile. Smile at the idea that a person could change so much without a shred of remorse in her heart.

The woman who used to shed tears upon learning that I was having a tough time in my government job, just said that she would message me back after I told her I almost died.

A few years back, Lieshaa sent me a picture containing a lengthy text while I was in the bank. It had been about a week since I started the job and was loaded with work. She felt that I had grown tired of her and was missing the talks we used to have every single day.

Here's the text that the image in question contained:

"I think one of the saddest things is when two people really get to know each other: their secrets, their fears, their favorite things, what they love, what they hate, literally everything, and then they go back to being strangers. It's like you have to walk past them and pretend like you never knew them, never even talked to them before, when really, you know everything about them."

I decided to send the same image to her. She opened the message, saw the image, and ignored it.

I was in a delusion for years on end. She made me believe that I was a knight in shining armor who had come to save her from what she claimed to be an abusive marriage. All I could see now in the mirror was the biggest clown to ever exist.

I had no idea why I was letting myself get humiliated by her every single day. Perhaps there was a part of me that still held hope that things were going to go back the way they were.

Meanwhile, I had started posting sad quotes, reels, and other grim stuff on social media. I had set my story privacy to custom and it was visible to two people: Lieshaa and Rahul.

After watching my stories for a few days, Rahul finally messaged me and asked me what had happened. I told him that the girl who was sitting beside me in the car that night had dumped me, and I was heartbroken. He spent a lot of time trying to cheer me up and pleaded with me to stop sharing sad quotes and images on social media.

As for Lieshaa, she didn't respond to any of the stories. She didn't care.

I was taking things too far, one step at a time. I didn't know what else to do. I was steadily growing tired of life. A few days later, I did something that I'm embarrassed about to this day.

I had had enough.

There was a time when I used to laugh at the idea of people seeking medical help to cure their depression. My mind couldn't fathom the idea that a depressed person would go to a doctor, take pills, and get cured.

Every day, I used to wake up in a dark room, take an hour to get up from bed, somehow finish my work, go back to sleep again, struggle to eat food and go back to sleep again at night. She had absolutely no idea what I was going through. She knew she held the power to change my life around in a split second, but I was old news to her by this point.

I couldn't take it anymore. I feared that I would do something drastic if I didn't talk to someone about my condition. That night, I sat my brother and mom down and told them everything.

Minus the part about Lieshaa being Rahul's wife.

The next day, I told Lieshaa that I was depressed and suicidal, and I had no choice but to go see a doctor. She seemed a bit worried over it but still didn't talk for long.

"I spend my days thinking about how it would feel waking up every morning and seeing your face. I sometimes end up crying and wonder why you didn't come into my life sooner. I think I'm going into depression."

These were the exact words she uttered four years ago while aggressively pursuing me and trying to make me understand that she couldn't live without me. She knew what depression was and how threatening it could be to a person's well-being.

Now that I had it, it was the least of her concerns.

An hour later, my brother drove me to a hospital that one of his friends had recommended to him. As soon as we reached the place, I was stunned.

Right in front of the hospital building, on the opposite side of the road, was the exact spot where I had met her for the very first time. The same spot where I picked her up on my bike three years ago.

Ours was one of the largest cities in India. And the hospital my brother took me to was right beside the spot where she first met me. Destiny had played a cruel joke on me.

I had come full circle.

The doctor prescribed me a bunch of pills and I took them regularly over the next two weeks. The pills were making me feel sleepy all the time. My entire work schedule had turned upside down. I was struggling to finish my work and would often doze off while typing on my laptop.

I decided against continuing the dosage. Meanwhile, she hadn't called or sent a single message, asking for an update on my visit to the doctor. This was the stuff of nightmares, where the person you trust with your life suddenly turns into the most heartless, evil being.

A few days passed. One morning, I finished writing some news pieces and was not in a condition to write more. I closed the laptop and it took less than a minute for me to fall into slumber.

When I woke up, I heard whispers near me. I decided to keep my eyes closed and not move an inch. My mom and my brother were sitting on his bed, talking.

They were worried. My brother was consoling her and pleading with her to stop crying. Never in her worst nightmares had she imagined seeing me in such a state. That night, I talked with her and told her that I had been experiencing improvement in my mental health over the past few days. I lied, but it was the least I could do to make her stop worrying.

I had never hated Lieshaa more.

One day, while scrolling YouTube, I stumbled upon the song "Love Me Like You Do." It immediately took me back to the night she sent me this very song and dedicated it to me.

As soon as I saw it, I couldn't hold back my tears. I immediately shut the door of my room to make sure no one saw me in that state.

I didn't know what came over me. I took out my phone and turned on the front camera. I recorded a message for her, crying uncontrollably for the entirety of the video.

"Liesh... what has happened to this relationship? Where are those days when you used to care? I miss 2018, Liesh... I was new, I was exciting, and you couldn't go a day without talking to me. I finally fell in love with you after realizing how much I meant to you. My love is still the same all these years later, but yours..."

I used to be a different person before meeting Lieshaa and falling in love with her in 2018. I fondly remember a girl who seemed interested in me back when I was in college, more than a decade ago. I was informed about the same by a few classmates, including the girl's close friends.

I wasn't interested, though. I always made it a point to keep our conversations strictly about classwork.

Now, I was sending a video of myself, crying like a pathetic loser, to someone who probably wouldn't care if I died tomorrow.

I had fallen off hard.

That night, she saw the video and left me on read. I couldn't sleep all night, while she did, without a care in the world. Lieshaa had taught me an important life lesson that night.

NEVER cry in front of a woman. It turns her off like nothing else.

By the next night, I had turned into an emotional wreck. I began messaging her repeatedly. I messaged her on every app she was on. I didn't stop here, though. I called her as well. About 15 times. None of the calls were received.

June 22, 2022, 12:32 a.m.

"What happened?" Her blunt, first message read. "Dude, I have a family... why are you creating problems? Why are you trying to destroy my family dude? My brother's here for a few days, and you... why are you forcing me? You're destroying my family... shit!"

I had dozed off by the time she sent the messages. I woke up the next day, as miserable and depressed as I had ever been, only to see those messages pop up on my screen. She had yelled at me.

"Dude."

After addressing me by my name for years on end, she called me "dude." I wasn't in a condition to boot up my laptop and work at that moment. All I could picture was that message of hers.

I typed my response with shaking hands. I sent about 20 messages, one after the other. After a few minutes, I realized that the woman had humiliated me enough.

I unsent every single message. It didn't matter anyway.

The Gift

After pondering on it for a few minutes, I turned on my phone screen and located the dating app that I had been using for two weeks now. I opened the app, removed the pictures I'd uploaded, and hit "delete account."

Shortly after Lieshaa's final message, someone suggested I should install a dating app to get over her. The pills didn't do much and I wasn't keen on increasing the dosage and possibly getting addicted to them.

"Why the hell not, let's try this as well," I said to myself.

Fast forward two days, and I was now chatting with a bunch of girls on the app. I ended up clicking with one of them.

Himani was quite possibly the most cheerful and carefree girl I had ever come across. We set up a date for the weekend and for the first time in months, I was looking forward to something. It seemed like it had been ages since I stepped out of the house.

After a fun game of bowling at the mall, we sat down in a corner of the adjoining restaurant. We spent a couple of hours talking about life, our likes and dislikes, past relationships, and career aspirations.

A few more dates followed. And then came the last one.

The two of us had gotten quite comfortable with each other by this point. On that fateful night, we were enjoying a horror movie at the theater. Minutes into the movie, she started playing with my hand, looking at me expectantly.

I knew where this was going. And I was beyond excited.

The movie hall was half-empty and was mostly filled with couples. The two of us were seated in a corner in one of the middle rows, with the nearest person being six seats away.

We kept looking at each other for the next few minutes, not caring one bit about the movie. I put my hands on hers and brought myself closer to her. The flashes emanating from the movie screen were illuminating on her face, making her look all the more pretty.

I finally made the move. Holding her chin with my hand, I brought her lips closer to mine, before gently kissing them. Himani grabbed my ears with both of her hands and made sure that our lips wouldn't part.

It hadn't even been 20 seconds since we began kissing when suddenly, I signaled for her to stop. I then rushed towards the washroom, leaving her dumbstruck and seemingly embarrassed. I looked in the mirror and could see a bit of her lipstick plastered on the side of my lower lip. I quickly rubbed it until it disappeared, before washing my face. I came back to the seat, profusely apologized to her, and asked if we could leave.

She was certainly pissed at me but was polite enough to suppress her anger. The next evening, she called me at her home. Her parents were abroad, visiting her older sister.

"I can't apologize enough for what happened yesterday," I said as soon as I entered her home. "I was just... I didn't kn--"

"Shhh! I completely get it. The way you were talking about that girl at the mall, I could see the pain in your eyes. I mean, it did hurt quite a bit when you moved away from me all of a sudden, but it's okay. It hasn't been long since you were dumped. Maybe it will take a few more months for you to get over her."

"I downloaded that app for the sole purpose of finding someone and moving on... and it felt like it did work when I met you. I guess I need more time," I said.

We hugged each other and promised to remain friends.

As I was leaving, she hugged me again, putting her mouth on my ear.

"It's not off the table, Abhilash. We could try again, somewhere down the line... if you manage to move on," she whispered, before kissing me on the cheek. I smiled at her, got in the car, and drove away.

As I was deleting my account, I began wondering, "Will I ever be able to move on from Lieshaa?"

My brother and I checked our bags one last time before zipping them up and putting on the locks. It was 2 a.m. and we had a flight to catch at 5.

Both of us had been history buffs since we were kids. Watching The History Channel all day while munching on cream biscuits used to be our favorite pastime during summer vacation back then.

He had been noticing for a while that I was still depressed as hell, and he was worried.

"We're heading to Egypt in a week," he told me out of the blue, a few weeks ago. Visiting The Great Pyramids of Giza had always been a dream of mine, and it was about to turn into reality very soon.

I couldn't have been happier. I needed this trip like a man lost in the desert would need an oasis. I was at the lowest point of my life. Even failing 12th grade and leaving the city in 2014 didn't affect me as much as Lieshaa's betrayal did. It was something that I KNEW was never going to happen.

I believed her too much.

The cab was here. It was pitch black outside. We quickly loaded the suitcases in the trunk of the cab and got inside. The two of us waved at our parents as the cab began driving away.

The cab exited the colony and was now approaching the nearest square. There was no other vehicle in sight. The silence of the night was quite soothing.

And then it hit me as soon as we reached the square. I realized that at this very moment, not more than two km from the square, she was lying on her bed, sleeping peacefully.

She had no idea that the guy she once dearly loved was on his way almost 5,000 km away, hoping to cure the depression that her betrayal had caused. Almost 10,000 km of to and fro travel... what if something happened? What if there was an accident up there? What would be her reaction? Would she even care? She hadn't cared when I almost choked to death, so why would she now?

The mind of a severely depressed person is a dark, dangerous, chaotic place.

It took a six-hour connecting flight to reach Cairo, Egypt. When we reached the hotel room, I suddenly recalled an incident we had after arriving at our hotel in Dubai, four years ago.

My brother and I had reached the hotel at 1 p.m. and quickly freshened up, before going out to get some food. We found an eatery inside a tiny complex and asked the server to make it a takeaway. We wanted to eat our food in peace in our hotel room.

"Drat," my brother yelled, as soon as we came back to our room.

"What happened?" I asked.

"The cold drink wasn't packed properly and it spilled everywhere. Everything inside the bag is now soggy."

The two of us were too tired at that point to go back and get more food. We hadn't eaten in hours and gobbled up the soggy food before hitting the bed.

That little, annoying incident in our hotel room in Dubai had become a precious memory now. Back when it happened, it was nothing more than an accident that mildly infuriated me. Four years later, now that I had lost Lieshaa, I would give anything to go back to that day. To that month. Or even to that year.

She still loved me back then.

We hit the bed as soon as we entered the hotel room. The hotel balcony had an insane view of the Pyramids, which were not more than three km ahead. It was one of the most beautiful sights my eyes had ever come across.

The next day, we arrived at the Pyramids complex. We walked all the way to the main hall inside the Great Pyramid, the biggest of the three. The tunnel that took us to the hall was incredibly narrow and was a claustrophobe's nightmare.

We rode a camel and took pictures everywhere, including the Sphinx, before leaving the complex. Right in front of the complex was a McDonald's and a KFC. Enjoying fried chicken in a KFC while staring at the 4,500-year-old Pyramids is still one of the coolest things I've ever done.

Lieshaa was on my mind all this while.

We spent the next three days traveling to other notable spots. On the final day, we headed to the airport in the morning. I noticed a jewelry shop at the Cairo Airport, beside which was a confectionery stall. I ended up buying a basket full of chocolates and candies.

A three-hour flight took us to Sharjah, where we had an hour-long layover.

The two of us hadn't eaten much in the morning and decided to get some food. The cafeteria was right in front of us.

The same Indian cafe that we ate at back in 2018, during our Dubai trip. As my brother was ordering two *dosas* for us, all I could think of was how times had changed for the worse.

There was an empty, tall stool right in front of the counter. He put the two *dosas* on it and we began eating. Four years ago, we stood at the same spot, eating *dosas*.

Four years ago. The summer of 2018.

I would give everything to go back to that time. Enjoying a dosa with my brother at the Sharjah Airport in 2018, awaiting Lieshaa's arrival in my life.

Life wasn't the same anymore. Everything had changed in the past four months. She couldn't give two shits about me now. And that realization hit me like a thousand knives stabbing me all over my body.

The next morning, we were back home. That very evening, I shared a bunch of pictures from our trip on my social media handles. Two days later, I expectantly checked the 100 or so likes that the pictures had received.

She hadn't liked it.

I tried to hide my sadness with a fake smile, recalling how she once used to be the first person to hit a like as soon as I posted anything.

"You didn't need to bring all of this, Abhi. It's too much," Rahul was reluctant to take the chocolates I had brought from the trip.

"Rahul, I know she's fond of chocolates. And these were duty-free. Please take all of them and don't worry one bit," I assured him.

I had called Rahul the next day to hand over the gifts that I bought for his daughter.

She loved chocolates. And so did Lieshaa.

It had been about 30 minutes since Rahul came. By this point, Lieshaa had called him three times, asking him to come back quickly. Every call of hers felt like a bullet in the chest.

While Rahul was about to leave, she called again. Her voice was faint but I could still make out what she was saying.

"Where are you?" she yelled.

"I'm about to leave. Sorry, I'll be there in 5," he replied calmly while smiling at me.

"Don't cut the call, and come back quickly," she ordered.

Rahul gave me another smile, thanked me for the gifts, and left.

At that moment, all I wanted was to be in his place. He was at my home, and his wife had been calling him repeatedly to come back. She knew I was sitting right beside him, and seeing her concern and care for him would break me even further. But she had stopped giving a damn a long time ago.

"I've never loved someone as much as you. Not even Rahul. Believe me."

I did. I believed her. And this is what I got. Seeing her call him right in front of me, shower him with all the care in the world. The fact that she was now actively trying to make me feel worse, knowing full well that I was severely depressed... I was on the verge of a nervous breakdown.

The woman who seemed like the sweetest, most caring, and innocent being in the world had taken off her mask. And all I could see beneath it was pure evil.

That night, I received a message from Lieshaa.

"These things are done only for someone with whom a person is in a relationship. These gifts... please, no need to do such things again. We're not in a relationship. Don't do this again, please."

I didn't respond.

I was stunned by the bluntness that was on display. By the sheer disregard of the pain that the person she once called her life was going through.

The next morning, she messaged again.

"Never do such things again, please."

There had to be a reason why she messaged twice. She could've simply ended it with last night's message but went out of her way to send another one in the morning. She definitely wanted to have a conversation.

Maybe things were about to come back to normal. Maybe, just maybe, the worst period of my life was finally about to come to an end. I still had feelings for her, even though I had lost a ton of respect for her over the past few months. But things could get better. I would forgive her in a jiffy if she was planning to come back to me.

"Are you serious?" I asked.

She didn't even open the message.

Two days had passed. There was no response from her. It was clear as day that she had deleted the conversation after reading my message from the notification panel.

Her aversion to me had hit an all-time high. The woman I loved more than anyone in the world didn't consider me important enough to open my message.

"We haven't talked in two days. This will keep happening more often until the day comes when you'll be too busy to even answer a message."

This was one of her messages that led to me quitting my government job back in 2018. I couldn't handle the fact that she was far away, crying relentlessly because I had left her again.

I cared enough about her to quit something for which I had worked tirelessly for a year.

And she didn't even open my message.

She had written her number in my book that I didn't see for five years. It was a scenario straight out of the movies. But reality had set in now. Real life isn't a movie.

She did fall in love with me.

She did write her number in the book.

She did promise me that now we were finally together, she wouldn't ever leave me.

And then she left.

Real life isn't a movie.

I had never been this helpless before. Who was this woman? This wasn't the Lieshaa who was madly in love with me. This was someone else.

This was hands down the most evil being I'd ever come across. She couldn't stoop any lower at this point.

I was dead wrong. I hadn't seen the worst of her yet.

She's Not Yours, It's Just Your Turn

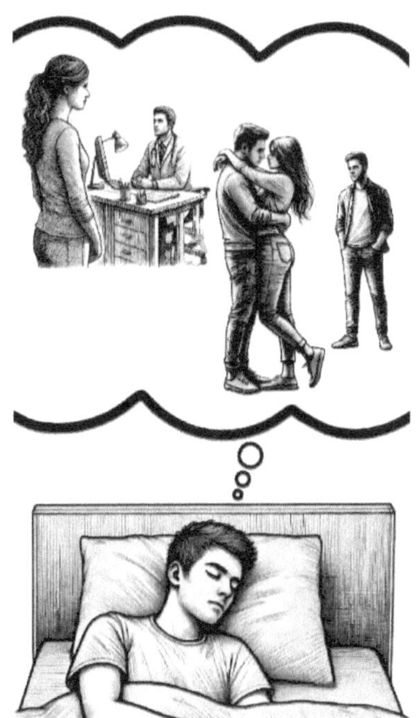

"Abhilash, an ant just bit me. Can you kiss it and make it okay?"

"Aww… here, Liesh…"

"Thanks, Abhi, it healed instantly. Idiot ant."

Idiot ant.

I couldn't help but giggle while recalling our text exchange from years ago. Lieshaa's sweet texts. A grown woman who was still an innocent child at heart. A woman with the purest soul in existence. A woman who could do no wrong. A woman who couldn't even hurt a fly.

Where did that woman go?

December 4, 2022, 11:13 a.m.

"I need help from you... I've never asked for anything but I seriously need your help now, please," her first message in five months read.

After Lieshaa didn't even open my message, my depression worsened. I knew I had lost her forever but all I could do was keep living, with the hopes that I would get over her someday.

And then, she messaged me again, out of the blue.

At first, I was beside myself with joy. Maybe she couldn't get me out of her mind and was now finally ready to come back to me. I was going through the worst phase of my life, had nothing to look forward to, and was still depressed as hell. I hadn't genuinely smiled since March.

When one doesn't have anything to look forward to in life, every single moment becomes a chore.

I would've done anything to become happy again, and accepting her back into my life was at the top of the list.

And then, it hit me. Let me paint you a picture.

This was quite possibly the most important message she had ever sent me. It taught me a lesson that I needed to learn.

A woman leaves you after promising the world to you for years on end. You cry, beg, and plead with her to come back. But her once gentle, pure heart is now hard as stone. You are depressed, suicidal, and almost choke to death.

She doesn't give a shit.

You send her gifts as a gesture of love, and she makes it clear that she doesn't want anything to do with you. You're now a nuisance to her. Your texts that once used to bring joy to her face, now leave her annoyed. For months on end, she lives her life to the fullest, sleeps like a baby, hangs out with her friends, laughs at their jokes, and eats well. The fact that you're out there, going through sleepless nights one after the other, is of no concern to her.

You could die tomorrow and she wouldn't bat an eyelid.

And then, she contacts you, FIVE MONTHS LATER.

Her very first message?

Not an apology. Not a bit of regret over destroying your life and leaving you a broken man. Not even a "Hey, are you okay?"

She immediately asks for help in the most blunt, straightforward manner possible.

This was an incredibly vile, disgusting, and nasty person that I was dealing with. She ignored me for what seemed like an eternity. And the moment she needed help, a light bulb went off in her mind.

"I've done the absolute worst to this man. But unlike me, he's probably still in love and I can use it to my advantage. I'll shamelessly message him and ask for help right away," she probably must've thought.

The entitlement of this evil witch was off the charts.

"My parents raised me like a princess. Never said no to me, no matter what I asked for."

I recalled how she once told me this while talking about her differences with Rahul and his family.

It all made sense now. Her entitlement came from years and years of never being told NO.

I, who once was the love of her life, the apple of her eye, the person with whom she had planned to spend her life, was now somebody she contacted ONLY BECAUSE she needed help. Deep down inside, I knew she wouldn't have messaged me if she didn't need help.

I wasn't angry anymore. I was sad. This was a woman who could do no wrong, had nothing but love and respect in her heart for me, and couldn't go a day without talking to me.

Now, all I could see was a cunning, heartless opportunist who wanted to exploit a guy because she knew he still loved her.

"It's a small help. Are you there?" she continued.

I didn't respond. I waited. Patiently.

"I'm bedridden. Can you do something for me? I urgently need Rs. 3500... can you send me the money? I'll return as soon as I get well. If you're willing to help... I really need the money. I'll return it soon, I promise."

Again, I didn't respond.

A clown with money in his bank account, stupid enough to hand it over the moment she asked for it. That's all she thought of me. And it hurt bad.

There's something about a person who makes it clear to you time and again that you don't matter to them one bit, and then asks for your help out of the blue.

There can't be a bigger turnoff.

Was she THIS oblivious to what she was doing? Or was she so entitled that she couldn't fathom that a man she broke from within would be pissed at her, seeing her come back ONLY because she needed some money?

"Everything I own is yours. Every single penny I've earned over the past three years is yours. The only reason I wake up and work is to make sure I will have enough when we're together and I can give you anything you ask of me."

It hadn't even been a full year since I told her that the sole purpose of my life was to ensure she was happy and that everything I owned belonged to her.

That was then.

Back then, she wasn't the diabolical, scheming, wicked being that she had become now. Or maybe she was but had somehow succeeded in making me believe that she was the most pure-hearted woman to ever exist.

The next morning, Lieshaa messaged me again. And she was livid.

"No matter how many times you called me to meet at your home, I came. I faced a million problems... he asked where I was going and I lied every single time. And now when I need your help, you're ignoring me? You selfish prick, all you ever wanted was to sleep with me. I hate you... I really needed the money, but an ungrateful guy such as you wouldn't understand," she wrote.

I didn't know where to begin. There was SO MUCH to unpack here.

The audacity of this woman.

I had grossly underestimated her. She was WAY craftier than I could've ever imagined.

Her attempt at gaslighting me into thinking that I was the only one who used to call her to meet me was a pathetic one. There were a couple hundred texts of hers on my phone, pleading with me to meet her.

She begged me to love her forever. To marry her. To give her a child. To take her away from the horrid life that she was living. I said yes to everything before she decided to dump me all of a sudden.

Now, she was claiming I only wanted to sleep with her. This woman that I once cherished as if she was a goddess, and the best thing to ever happen to me, turned out to be a sleazy tramp.

Not too long ago, I would've cried my heart out upon reading that message. But now, I had gotten numb. I just didn't care. We both knew she was lying in hopes of guilt-tripping me into giving her some money.

But I had already come to the realization that this wasn't a movie. This was real life.

She wasn't the sweet angel she once pretended to be. She was, without a shadow of a doubt, the most evil person I had ever met. I wasn't going to be the bigger person by forgiving her and giving her the money. I was going to treat her the way she deserved to be treated.

"How are you?" She continued. "How long has it been, Abhi?"

I finally sent my first response to her. A screenshot of our last conversation where she told me that it was over, before refusing to open my text. That was five months ago.

"So, are you gonna keep whining about the past instead of letting go? People fight all the time. Why would you want to end the relationship for such ridiculous reasons? Are you still in the city?"

I had no words.

God I HATED this woman. With every fiber of my being.

I once loved this woman with all my heart. I helplessly watched as she turned into the most despicable being. I had now realized that my feelings towards her were purely sexual at this point.

Lieshaa was the most beautiful woman I had come across. She was also the sweetest, kindest, and most loving woman I had ever met.

She was still insanely pretty.

Sweet, kind, and loving? Absolutely not.

All of a sudden, I began seeing her as a physical object of sexual desire, and nothing more than that.

She made me feel like the most worthless human to ever exist.

I wanted her to feel the same.

"Yep, sleep..." I wrote.

"What??" she asked, confused.

"Sleep. I did want to sleep with you. There was no love from my end. Why the hell would I fall in love with a characterless wench, who was cheating on her husband with me? But I do want to sleep with you again," I responded. I wanted to hit her where it hurt the most.

"What? Idiot! Duffer! Your mind... it's completely ruined. There's nothing left in it except lust."

The woman who once couldn't keep her hands off me was now hurling insults over being asked to do the same again.

"Fuck off," I replied.

"What are you doing? Are you still in the city? Are you busy? I'm sick, bedridden at home," she said, ignoring my foul language.

"Yes or no?

"Hmm... yes. But do one thing. I need some time, I was told to take ample rest. I'm not well. Please believe me, I'm not lying," she shamelessly lied.

She kept sending messages one after the other over the next three days.

"Do you miss me?"

"Had dinner?"

"Good night!"

"Traveled anywhere lately?"

I had no idea why she was interested in me all of a sudden. I was stuck between wanting to throw the absolute worst profanities known to mankind at her and treating her well in hopes of getting her back.

I chose the former. The rage that had built up over the past five months needed venting immediately.

"Listen, sis. Why are you wasting my time? If you want to hook up like you used to back in the day, come over. Or else, go find another sheep to slaughter. I know you have plenty of guys wanting to sleep with you in your inbox at this very moment. Go have fun. Do what you do best. I seriously don't give a damn. I've already moved on from your treacherous ass."

"I hate you too. Bye forever... don't ever show your face." she was livid. "Who do you think I am, a tramp or something? I hope you're happy after treating me in such a manner. I can't believe I used to think you were a good person. Unfollowing you."

A week passed.

One afternoon, she messaged again. And my worst fear came true.

"Bro, did you really think I needed you? I have someone special in my life. He always cares for me, supports me, and helps me in my time of need. You, on the other hand, are selfish. Please, make sure you never show your face again. Atul is his name."

"Are you serious?" I asked. I had a sinking feeling inside me as soon as she mentioned another guy's name.

"Yeah... I love him to death. He's a doctor and is very caring."

"💔," I replied.

She didn't respond.

She had to be telling the truth. She was pissed. She had waited for about a week before sending another message. A woman with her looks would always have an army of men in her DMs, waiting for that one chance to strike. And it seemed like sometime during the past week or so, one of them got lucky.

"Lieshaa was never mine, it was just my turn," I mumbled to myself. "Now, it's someone else's."

I was a clown to believe that a woman who betrayed her husband for me would never betray me for another man. I had broken my friend's trust and karma had finally come calling.

I got out of bed, approached my bookshelf, and opened the bottom drawer. With tears in my eyes, I put the first stack of books on the side, revealing a tiny box placed on a shorter stack. I wondered if she was making the same promises to him that she once made to me. Rs. 3500! That's all it took for her to start showering her love upon someone else.

I opened the box.

The ring worth Rs. 1.91 lac that I had purchased from the jewelry shop at the Cairo Airport was securely placed inside, shining brilliantly.

A Letter Written in Tears

January 20, 2023, 8:40 p.m.

"I'm in the hospital. You can ask Rahul, he'll tell you everything," her message popped up on Instagram. I didn't respond. At this point, I had stopped trusting her completely. I didn't call Rahul as well.

A few hours passed. At about midnight, he messaged me.

"She's here." Rahul messaged me. "Our second baby daughter!"

A storm had broken loose in my mind. My heart wasn't being able to comprehend the dark reality that was before me. All I could think of was our very first conversation on that fateful day of August 3, 2018.

"Abhilash... I need to pick up my daughter from her playschool. Bye, and take care..."

When Lieshaa contacted me for the first time in 2018, we had a quick conversation. It ended when she told me she needed to pick up her daughter from the playschool.

She now had another daughter. Soon, she will start attending playschool as well. Every day, Lieshaa will get ready, get on her moped, and bring her back from the playschool. This time around, though, she won't be telling me about it. I'm not a part of her life anymore, nor will I ever be. She doesn't have my number saved. She doesn't even think of me at all.

The realization hit me like a ton of bricks.

It was all over. The last glimmer of hope I had, had died down. I began doing calculations in my head before opening his message.

Lieshaa left me in March 2022.

In May, when she was a little over one month pregnant, she said the following to me about the two of us possibly having a kid, *"Whatever it is, it will be ours, Abhi."*

She gave me hope while her pregnancy had already begun.

I suddenly recalled her mentioning the name, Atul. She told me he was a doctor. Could... could it be that he was the doctor that she was seeing during her pregnancy? Did she fall in love with him while paying visits to the hospital? I never got the answer.

I congratulated Rahul on the baby's arrival.

"We were hoping for a boy," he wrote. After having a daughter, they were expecting their second child to be a boy.

"I would have been the happiest man in the world with having a baby with that woman, no matter if it was a boy or a girl," I thought to myself.

I spent the next few minutes explaining to him how girls are way better than boys in many aspects. He needed to be in high spirits after the baby's arrival and I did my best to cheer him up.

The next morning, I had finally made a decision.

It had been almost a year. I still hadn't gotten over her one bit. No matter what I was doing, the only constant in my mind was her face. I loved her. I hated her. I wished she was mine. I wished she would drop dead. I was ashamed of the evil thoughts running in my mind.

It was all over anyway. What seemed like the perfect love story to me was just a case of a bored housewife wanting to have some short-term fun behind her husband's back. She had her fun and was now ready to focus on her family.

But what about the thousands of promises that she had made to me over those four years? Every such message of hers was now haunting me and there didn't seem to be an end in sight to this torment.

"You had big hopes for me, wanted to see me bring someone home, marry her, and have little, adorable kids. Instead, I'm a depressed mess of a person. The woman I fell in love with HATES me, and is now having the time of her life with her husband and her two kids.

"I will spend the rest of my life dreaming about how happy I would have been if she had kept her promises. I will keep having nightmares of the reality I now face: seeing her live happily, while she knows what I'm going through, and doesn't care one bit.

"I wish I had never met her. I wish I had done a ton of things differently. But it's too late at this point. I tried to be a good son and a good brother, and I hope that I made you proud at least a few times over the years.

I'm fully aware of how selfish I am and what my passing will do to all of you, but I'm helpless at this point. I'm a broken man. I live every day for the sake of living. I don't enjoy doing anything. Nothing at all. Every single moment of my life is worse than the previous one. I want you to know that this is the only thing that can help me be at peace.

I'm terribly sorry. I love you."

Abhi.

I had finished writing the final paragraphs of the letter. The five-page letter that my family was going to read after my passing.

Over the years, I had read countless news pieces about people ending their lives. I never understood how a person could reach a point where the only option left for them was to commit suicide. How someone had the guts to kill themselves and end their precious life. How they didn't care one bit about the people they would leave behind.

It all made sense to me now.

I waved goodbye to my brother before heading inside the airport. It was the morning of April 5, 2023. I was on my way to Bangkok, Thailand.

Alone. Solo.

I had always dreamed of traveling solo. The idea of getting on a plane and spending a few days in a far-off country, with not a single familiar face in sight, had always intrigued me.

There were a bunch of things I needed to check off my bucket list before ending it all.

Traveling solo was one of those things. The last one would be celebrating my 32nd birthday with my family. A couple of days after spending one last happy moment with my family, I was going to end my life.

I hadn't felt this calm and relaxed in ages. I had a great nap during the four-hour flight that reached Bangkok at 1:30 a.m. As soon as I came out of the airport, I booked a cab and got in. The hotel was about 30 minutes away. Since it was way past midnight, I didn't see many vehicles for almost the entirety of the ride.

At one point, I put my head out the window as soon as I saw a flyover ahead. For the next two minutes or so, I kept staring at the beautiful, dark night sky and the sparkling skyscrapers in the distance, while taking deep breaths.

I reached the hotel at 2:15 a.m. As soon as I entered my room, I threw my backpack and suitcase in a corner, took my clothes off, headed to the bathroom, and got under the shower. I didn't budge an inch for the next 10 minutes and took it all in.

It had been a little over a year since Lieshaa left me. I had learned a lot of things over the past 13 months, but one thing stood out.

After I was dumped, I began appreciating the little things in life. Things that wouldn't have caught my attention if I was still happy, had now become intriguing all of a sudden.

The flowers in our garden, clean bedsheets, the chirping of birds in the morning, a hot shower, a long walk after dinner, a good night's sleep, and much, much more. These simple pleasures of life had suddenly become so much more important to me.

After coming out of the shower, I stood beside the bed for a little while. Deathly quiet outside. I was alone, in a small, dimly-lit hotel room, 4200 km away from my home, family, and friends.

And her.

I hit the bed without checking my phone. It was already past 2:30 and I had to move to a nearby hostel in a few hours.

That night, I dreamed about Lieshaa. A completely random dream. All I remembered was her dog playing with me while she smiled at him from a distance. This wasn't the first time. Over the past year or so, I had dreamed about her countless times. All of these dreams had one thing in common.

She didn't speak a single word to me in any of them.

I spent the next two days visiting some of Bangkok's most popular spots. On the third day, I spent about nine straight hours at the hostel pool party, meeting new people, clicking tons of pictures, and chilling in the pool.

And then came the final night. I took a cab to King Power Mahanakhon, Bangkok's tallest building. I reached there at about 10 and hurried towards the ticket counter. The lift took less than a minute to reach the 77th floor. I then entered another, larger lift that finally brought me to the roof.

The circular roof had a large platform in the middle. It housed massive couches on each of its 10 or so steps. At the top, there was an open space where visitors could sit back and relax or enjoy the breathtaking view of the city. The area surrounding the platform had a massive bar, DJ, tables and couches in every corner, and a glass-floored observation deck.

I took the free mocktail included with the ticket and began walking around. The DJ was playing an incredibly soothing track, adding to the relaxed atmosphere on the roof. I couldn't last more than a few seconds on the glass floor. My fear of heights kicked in and I immediately got off the floor, taking a sigh of relief.

I then decided to head over to the top of the platform. Upon reaching the top, I simply stood there, looking into the distance, and taking in the magnificent view of Bangkok at night.

I could see thousands of shimmering lights in every direction, beneath the quiet, velvet sky. The beautiful skyline stretched into the distance, beyond which there was nothing but utter darkness of the city's outskirts. Strong gushes of wind tugged at my hair and clothes.

It was a view one could never get tired of.

I took a glance at the area surrounding the platform. Couples, families, friends... everyone was having a great time, talking to each other, clicking pictures, and making memories that were going to last a lifetime.

I couldn't help but imagine Lieshaa standing right beside me at that very moment. It would have been a moment to cherish till the very end. The two of us together, staring at the beautiful city from the top of its tallest skyscraper. A dream that would have turned into reality had she kept her promise. A dream that we used to see while looking into each other's eyes. A dream that had now become a living nightmare.

I stood in the same spot for quite some time, taking it all in. I then made a quick video call to my family to show them the Bangkok skyline. After taking one final look at the beautiful, glistening city, I headed towards the lift. A few minutes later, I was downstairs, walking away from the building. These past few days were going to stay with me for the rest of my life, whatever was left of it.

The next night, I was back home. Although I was hesitant about solo travel at first, it turned out to be one of the most fulfilling experiences of my life. Living in the moment, learning about other cultures, and moving at my own pace were just a few of the many things I learned while traveling solo.

I spent the next five months checking stuff off my bucket list.

• Called almost every close friend of mine and talked to each one of them for at least 10 minutes.

• Visited my mom's village where I used to spend my summer vacations. The last time I visited was way back in 2008 and the village had now turned into a developed town.

• Distributed food to 20 homeless people.

• Began spending more time with my family, something I hadn't done in years.

• Contacted Vani. Apologized profusely for the way I treated her that night, five years ago. She was now married and had a child. Had shifted to another state.

August was almost on the horizon.

In about two months, I was going to end it all. Nothing much was left for me to do except one thing, which was to celebrate one last birthday with my family.

On August 1, I came across a massive announcement on Twitter. Being a huge fan of professional wrestling, I couldn't believe my eyes when I saw that a major event was going to be held in Hyderabad, India, on September 8, 2023.

The timing couldn't have been better!

I had been a big fan since 2002 and always dreamed of attending a show. And now, mere weeks before ending my life, I had the opportunity to fulfill my wish.

August 3, 2023, 12:00 p.m.

Ajit was here in India for a rare two-week trip. We first met on my very first day of college and instantly became friends. He had been working in the US for quite some time now and had come to India after four years.

We entered the college premises and the guard asked us to put our contact numbers in the register. "Put in the details while I park the car," I asked Ajit.

A wave of nostalgia hit me as soon as I parked the car and stepped outside. So much had happened on this campus back in 2010-14. I had spent some of the best years of my life in this place. My eyes suddenly turned to a corner of the parking lot. Once an empty space, it now housed a full-fledged canteen.

It was the same spot where I used to always park my bike. The spot where I stood when she saw me for the very first time, a decade ago.

She wasn't in my life back then.

10 years later, after everything we went through, I had come full circle. She wasn't in my life, again.

Ajit and I spent the next hour or so roaming around the campus and visiting our classrooms. I entered my seventh-semester classroom and sat down on the chair that I used to sit alone on after my friends failed a year. I was alone, helpless, didn't have anyone to talk to, and depressed. I had no idea that at that very moment, a book lay on my shelf at home, with someone's number hidden inside.

Someone who cared. Someone who loved me. And now, she didn't anymore.

I then walked towards the back of the college. There it was. The large gate was partially opened and I could see the road that stood right ahead of it. I passed through the gate and stopped right at the spot where I once met Rahul and Lieshaa.

The smile on her face when she glanced at me that day was lost somewhere in time.

Never to return.

I took a deep sigh, took one last look at the road, and headed back to the campus.

That evening, I booked two front-row tickets to the wrestling event in Hyderabad. My brother and I were going to have the time of our lives. I was going to enjoy every single moment of the show since it would be one of our last memories together.

Losing a Son

My bucket list had just two items left in it now: watching a pro-wrestling event live and celebrating one final birthday with my loved ones.

I was aware of the never-ending pain and grief that I was about to leave my family with. I knew they would be devastated, numb, and regretful for the rest of their lives. But I was too selfish to care. All I wanted was to put an end to the torment that I had been enduring since Lieshaa's betrayal.

I had nothing to look forward to in life. The pain was too strong. I was looking forward to not waking up every single day, wondering why she did what she did. There was absolutely nothing that could stop me at that point.

It had been a few days since I booked the tickets. It was 4 in the afternoon and I had finished my workout mere minutes ago. I vividly remember seeing my father hurriedly leave the house, get into the car, and drive away while I was working out.

As I was about to head over to the kitchen to prepare a banana shake, I heard footsteps approaching my room. The door suddenly opened and in came my father. He was sweating profusely, breathing heavily, and I could see tears streaming down his face.

"Ayan has committed suicide," he said while looking at my brother, his entire body trembling.

"What?" my brother jumped off his bed, visibly shaken. I couldn't utter a single word. I kept looking at them with horror in my eyes.

Ayan was the 21-year-old son of my father's childhood friend, who lived a few blocks away.

My father then ran into the bedroom to wake my mom up. Mere seconds later, they rode away to his friend's home.

"Abhi!" my brother yelled at me, bringing me back to reality. I hadn't spoken a word since my father barged in. My mind was a mess and I still couldn't believe what had just happened.

He told me to change my clothes, before heading to the washroom. I quickly changed my clothes, washed my face, and began waiting for him to come out.

And then, I experienced one of the most heartbreaking moments of my life.

My brother came into the room. His eyes had turned red. He was in tears.

"Please, for the love of God... I'm begging you. Please, don't ever think of doing something like this. It's been more than a year since your breakup but I still feel that you haven't gotten over it. And now... I'm... I'm scared. If you ever think of harming yourself, just let us know and we'll do everything we can to make you feel better. But ple--"

"STOP CRYING!" I cut him off. "I've never once thought of such a thing. I'd never do such a thing. Why the hell would I take my life for a woman who won't give a crap if I die tomorrow? Trust me, and don't ever worry about me doing something drastic."

He was the strongest person I had ever known. I don't even remember the last time I saw him cry. There's no worse feeling than seeing your loved one shed tears, especially when they rarely show such strong emotions.

It's an indication that they are dead serious about what's bothering them.

I could see the fear in his eyes. I could sense the sadness in his voice. He was genuinely scared that I would do something irreversible, destroying our family in the process.

I kept assuring him as he wiped his tears off.

A year ago, I heard my mom cry while talking to my brother about my declining mental health. I still decided to end my life, knowing full well what would happen next. And now, I was seeing my brother cry in front of me.

At that moment, I imagined dragging Lieshaa out of her home, bringing her here, and making her watch the damage that she had caused. There was nothing but pure, unadulterated hatred in my heart for that woman. The people for whom I could give my life had turned into emotional messes because of her actions.

Lieshaa's lies had brought me to the verge of suicide. She had put me through so much pain that all I could think of was ending it all without caring about the tragic aftermath. I had become selfish to such an extent that I didn't even think of the well-being of people who had spent their lives supporting me through thick and thin. I was going to end my life for someone who left me broken and crying. She wouldn't give a damn, while the ones who were concerned for me would suffer till the end of their lives.

I wasn't lying to my brother.

The tears in his eyes. The concern on his face. The vulnerability that he had never displayed before. I couldn't put my family through it. I had to think beyond myself.

I had to keep living. Start afresh. Succeed. Be happy again.

For them.

I had firmly decided that I wasn't going to harm myself. It was as if a massive burden had suddenly been lifted off my shoulders. I was going to witness some incredibly horrifying scenes in a matter of minutes, making me realize that I had made the right decision.

We locked the home and headed to the last block of the colony. A large crowd had gathered in front of the home and we could hear faint cries that got louder as we approached closer. My brother and I stood at one side of the gate upon reaching. We saw many familiar faces but were too stunned to speak even a single word. All we managed to do was nod at each other while the cries grew louder with each passing second.

He had hanged himself.

His sister was inconsolable. She was screaming, crying, and yelling at her relatives to bring him back. Shortly after, a cab appeared in the distance. It stopped right in front of their home. Two men stepped out, followed by Ayan's mom. They held her firmly, as she was in no condition to stand on her own. She had just returned from the hospital, where the doctors had declared her 21-year-old son dead.

Her face was white as snow. It showed absolutely no emotions and had dried up after about an hour of incessant crying.

As soon as she was brought inside, her daughter lunged at her, held her with both of her hands, and began pleading with her, "He is okay, right? Mom, please say he's okay!"

Her mom couldn't take it anymore and burst into tears. At that moment, the daughter knew that her brother was never coming back. For the next several minutes, all I could hear from inside was the collective wailing of the duo.

I then saw another car approaching the house. At this point, about a hundred people had gathered in front of the house. Ayan's father stepped out of the car, walking slowly towards his home. His daughter came running out and hugged him, while he simply stood there, dejected, defeated, crushed. The heartbreaking visual was too much for me to handle. With tears in my eyes, I asked my brother if we could leave. He informed my parents that we were leaving before we began walking away from the house.

The screams and cries were fading with each step we took until I could hear nothing.

The next morning, I finished my work quickly as we had to attend the funeral. When I reached the house, I saw a massive crowd surrounding it. A large tent was set up in front of the house, and an empty bed stood in the middle.

It was silent in there. The men waiting outside were quiet, and so were the women sitting inside. It was only a matter of minutes, though, before the inevitable.

An Omni emerged in the distance, steadily making its way towards the house. I could see a bunch of men sitting inside, including Ayan's father.

 As soon as the car stopped, it started.

A sound that gives me chills to this day. A sound I've had nightmares about. A sound that will haunt me for the rest of my life.

There's a massive difference between a person dying of old age and a young guy taking his life at 21. When an old person passes away, the family of the deceased person is aware that they lived a long and fruitful life. When a person leaves this world at a young age, there's absolutely nothing one can do to comfort their family.

Ayan's mom and sister, as well as every single woman in there, broke down as soon as the body was brought out of the van. His mom and sister were screaming as loudly as they possibly could, while their loved one's body was placed in front of them, draped in white. Their eyes were red and swollen. They couldn't stop trembling and shaking. They were gasping for breath.

An hour later, my brother and I were heading home in our car after attending the funeral. Our parents were going to come back later as they wanted to stay for a while and console the grieving family.

It was a quiet ride. We weren't our usual talkative selves. Deep down inside, I knew. He was still scared. A part of him still feared for me. I needed to assure him. I didn't want him to worry at all.

"I swear on all three of you," I said while looking at him with a smile on my face. "There's no way I will ever try to harm myself in any way. Take a look at this."

I showed him a picture of Vani.

Vani, the girl who once begged me to come back to her. Who was now married and had a child. Who lived thousands of km away from here.

I lied to him. I told him that I had found someone special again. His eyes immediately lit up. His grim face had suddenly changed into a cheerful one.

He knew. A person who finds love again is less likely to think about the one who left him. He has finally moved on. He won't think about harming himself anymore.

It had worked. The lie had worked like a charm. My brother was content. He was happy. That's all I wanted.

A woman came into my life, loved me like no one else, begged me to love her back, made me the most beautiful promises, pleaded with me to take her away somewhere far from her sad, agonizing life, and ended it all when I was on the verge of making her dream come true.

A dream, which at that point, had become mine as well. Before she crushed it to pieces.

Ayan's body, placed on the funeral pyre. That was going to be me in a few weeks. My parents and brother would have been letting out uncontrollable cries and haunting screams, helplessly staring at my lifeless body.

I was going to make a grave mistake. I was incredibly close to destroying our little, happy family.

Suddenly, it struck me. What if I had gone ahead with the suicide?

I could picture it in my mind.

Lieshaa, who had brought me to the verge of suicide, would be sitting on her couch, smiling at her toddler who would be playing with her toys on the floor. Rahul would return home after picking up his daughter from school, change clothes, and lie down on the couch. Lieshaa would then bring her kids' favorite sweets from the kitchen and hand them over to the duo. Rahul would then switch on the TV and tune into the sports channel. The couple would then enjoy a game of IPL, with their kids gorging on sweets. Lieshaa would remember me as a moron who ended his life instead of moving on. She certainly wouldn't shed a single tear over the passing of someone she once "couldn't live without."

She would be happy. Content. Hopeful. Not a care in the world. She would sleep soundly every night, with no remorse in her heart.

On the other hand, my parents and brother would be broken inside, crying for days, possibly weeks on end. They wouldn't sleep or eat properly. They would spend every day asking me why did I leave. They would wonder if they could've done something more to prevent my death. They would look back at the time they spent with me, and yearn for those moments to come back. They would turn into shells of their former selves. They would never heal. Never have a genuine smile on their faces again.

They would be heartbroken. Miserable. Depressed. They would never experience true happiness again. They would keep regretting my death till the last moments of their lives.

A cold-hearted, self-centered, emotionally corrupt woman like Lieshaa would live a fulfilling life while my family would suffer for the rest of their lives.

There was no way in hell I was going to let that happen. That evening, I took the letter out of my shelf, where I had hidden it months ago. I walked up the stairs until I reached the terrace. I tore the letter into several pieces. I kept tearing it up until all I had left were little pieces of paper, hundreds of them.

I put the pieces in my pocket, intending to throw them in the dustbin after going downstairs. I walked up to a corner of the terrace and looked into the distance. About two km ahead, she stood somewhere inside her home. Calm, happy, probably chatting with someone new, telling him the same lies she once told me. Sending him a picture of hers in a lingerie, telling him that she's his, forever.

Our lives were about to change forever, very soon.

I was going to tell Rahul everything about us.

"Hey... Remember Me??"

I came downstairs, dumped the torn pieces of what was once a suicide letter into the dustbin, and headed to the dining room.

"I was thinking..." I said to my mom, after taking a chair. "What if all four of us go to the wrestling event in Hyderabad?"

She immediately said yes!

No one in my family loved pro-wrestling as much as I did. That didn't mean, though, that they wouldn't have liked attending a live event and watching the most popular wrestlers in the world up close.

The events that had happened over the past couple of days left a lasting impact on me. Not only did I change my mind about ending my life, but also realized the importance of family and doing everything I could to make them happy.

They were there for me during the darkest period of my life. I needed to do everything I could to make them happy. And what better way to do that than to take them to a rare wrestling event?

The moment my mom said yes to my idea, I realized how incredibly selfish I had been before. As soon as the tickets were made available, I had booked two for me and my brother. I even informed my mom about the trip and she couldn't have been happier.

Deep down inside, though, my parents yearned to join us on the trip and watch the event. But they didn't utter a word. They were happy to see us travel, enjoy the event, come back, and tell us all about it.

I hated myself for almost depriving them of the enjoyment of watching a wrestling spectacle live. Thankfully, I had realized my grave mistake before it was too late.

I didn't say another word and took my phone out. It took me less than a minute to book two more seats for the event, though they were a couple of rows behind us. Every seat in the front two rows had already been filled.

My mom immediately called my father to inform him that we were going to Hyderabad. The excitement on her face was priceless.

I slept well that night.

The event was held inside a small stadium with a capacity of 5000 people. As expected, the show was packed. Not a single seat was empty. It had been six long years since a show had been held in India. The crowd was LOUD for the entirety of the three-hour spectacle.

It featured some of the most well-known wrestlers on the planet, including John Cena, Rhea Ripley, Seth Rollins, and The Great Khali. We got to see them up close and it was unreal.

That night, at the hotel, my parents were beside themselves with excitement.

"John Cena looks like a legit movie star," my mom said. She was surprised when I told her that he was done as a full-time pro-wrestler years ago and was a movie star now.

"When's the next time they're coming to India?" my father asked expectantly.

I didn't have the slightest idea. But I was happy. As happy as I had been in ages. I couldn't believe I was going to let them stay at home while my brother and I would have one of the best experiences of our lives.

Booking those two extra tickets was one of the best decisions I'd ever made.

"Is there something that has been stressing you lately?" The doctor asked. "The report isn't anywhere close to alarming, but you do have a blood pressure slightly higher than normal."

"I did suffer from severe depression last year. I've been okay for quite some time now, though," I replied.

It had been a week since our trip to Hyderabad. While working on my laptop that morning, I suddenly felt a sharp pain in my chest. I informed my brother about it and we immediately headed to the hospital.

The doctor assured me that I was fine. He did point out, though, that my blood pressure was a bit higher than normal. He prescribed me some pills and advised me to reduce my daily egg yolk intake which was a part of my post-gym diet.

I was scared out of my wits.

While returning home, I asked my brother to stop the car at the side of the road. I got out of the car as soon as it stopped.

"What happened?" he asked, visibly confused.

"Nothing, I need some fresh air for a minute," I said.

I was standing right in front of the project workshop that Rahul and I used to visit back in the day. The workshop's shutters were down. It seemed like it hadn't been opened in ages. Possibly closed permanently. I then looked at the opposite side of the road. The coconut water kiosk wasn't there anymore. A grocery shop stood in its place.

Lieshaa, sitting on Rahul's bike, sipping coconut water, staring at me, nothing but love and admiration in her eyes... all of it was lost in time.

While I was destroying the suicide letter and staring in the direction where Lieshaa's home stood, something struck my mind.

We were together for four years. FOUR YEARS.

She came into my life, begged me to be hers, swore on her mom that she loved me after I rejected her, convinced me that her married life was nothing short of torturous, and pleaded with me to marry her, give her a kid, and take her away from here.

And then, she dumped me out of the blue.

After she was done with me, her feelings towards me suddenly changed. I no longer meant anything to her. I got depressed, took pills, cried, begged, requested her to take me back, and was on the verge of ending my life.

She couldn't care less.

I spent months wondering how a woman could change to such an extent that the one she considered her everything, now didn't mean shit to her. But I had no answer. She didn't give one.

I was miserable to the point that I almost ended my life, a move that would have destroyed three other lives. On the other hand, she was living her best life, having absolutely no regrets. It felt as if she had had her fun and wanted to focus on her family now.

She didn't consider one thing though.

She wasn't playing with a toy. I wasn't an inanimate object. She lied to a real, living, breathing person for years on end before getting bored and throwing him out of her life.

A long time ago, I once instructed Lieshaa to always delete our chats to make sure Rahul didn't find out about us. Looking back now, I couldn't help but laugh at how things had changed so drastically.

I had made the decision. I was well aware of the fact that the consequences would be dire. I once saw Rahul aggressively grab my friend and almost beat the crap out of him for cracking a joke about his wife. I could feel a chill run down my spine, wondering what he would do to me.

But at that point, my hatred for Lieshaa had long surpassed my fear of what Rahul would do to me. She had destroyed my life with her lies and was living hers as if nothing had happened. As if she was still the kind, gentle, and sweet soul she pretended to be for years.

I had been wanting to wait for a while before telling him everything about us. I wanted to spend a few months, enjoying life to the fullest. There was no telling what Rahul would do once he found out about us.

And then, the doctor's appointment happened. I had been reading and watching reports of people collapsing and passing away for months on end at that point. It had become a norm since the COVID-19 pandemic started. There was a part of me that believed I was going to meet the same fate.

And it could come at any time. The very next second. A few months down the line. Maybe, after several years.

I couldn't risk waiting.

The last thing I wanted was for me to suddenly pass away without letting Rahul know that she wasn't the flawless, caring, kind-hearted angel that she pretended to be.

I was an evil person through and through. I was well aware of that. Lieshaa and I betrayed my friend and her husband. Only one of us suffered consequences, though.

I couldn't live with that.

But before telling Rahul everything, I needed to talk with her one final time.

"Hey... remember me??"

I hit send.

These were the exact words she had messaged me on August 3, 2018, when this nightmare truly began. I hadn't messaged her since she told me about the doctor she had fallen in love with, back in December 2022. But I couldn't wait anymore now.

She did open WhatsApp but didn't open the message.

I once read somewhere that no response is also a response. And a powerful one. She didn't give a shit. She had stopped caring more than a year ago.

The next night, I sent another message to her.

"Hey... remember me??"

No response.

I was being ignored by someone who once promised me that our love was never going to die. I didn't stop, though.

"Hey, can you at least tell me one thing? I still sometimes read every single text of yours where you made all the promises in the world to me. You assured me that we were inseparable. And then, BAM! You mercilessly dumped me and since then, you've been pretending as if I don't even exist. Have you no shame?"

A notification popped up a few minutes later. She had finally responded.

"But nothing's changed. We're still the same. We're still in love," the tramp wrote.

"YOU LYING, DECEIVING SORRY EXCUSE OF A WOMAN!"

It had been 18 months since she dumped me.

It had been 13 months since she told me that our relationship was dead.

It had been 10 months since we last talked.

And she dared to tell me that we were still in love.

"I have a baby now. I've lost my looks. I've gained weight. You'll find someone else."

"I never cared about your looks. I loved you for what you were on the inside or pretended to be. I loved you so much... I believed every promise of yours. I never looked at other women while you were out there two-timing me. The bottom line is that you kept me on the hook for four years, you evil, inconsiderate piece of trash. And then you threw me away like what we had didn't mean shit to you. What makes me sad is that you'll never experience the kind of suffering that I did and still do.

"You and I, we aren't too different. We are two evil people who betrayed the same man. But why is it that I'm the only one who's suffering while you're living a happy, peaceful life?" I asked her.

"Abhi, trust me. I'm suffering too. I'm living a horrible, agonizing life. I was threatened with divorce the moment my second daughter was born. I cried all night but to no avail. We still fight. We fight all the time. We bring up each other's deceased parents, curse them, throw insults at them. When he brought up my parents, I couldn't take it anymore and ended up insulting his parents.

"He's made my life a living hell. I've been hit. On the face, like I once told you. I'm miserable. I'm seriously thinking about filing a case against him. I'm a woman and the Indian law favors us. We run the show. One complaint accusing a man of mental and physical torture is all it needs for the police to throw him in jail."

She had a history of lying. Lying to my face. She was probably throwing her husband under the bus to gain sympathy from me.

"And how is it my problem?" I had no sympathies left for someone who didn't give a crap when I was suffering. "How does that justify or relate to you ruining my life with your lies?"

She had no answer.

"I was about to kill myself after my birthday. I had written a letter addressed to my family. But something happened that made me change my decision.

"And you know what? It breaks my heart, realizing what you are thinking right now while reading this message. 'He should've killed himself. He was so close to doing it. He didn't, and now I'm being forced to listen to his sob stories.'

"I wanted to tell you something for quite some time now. Check this out," I wrote, before sending a picture.

It was the ring I had bought for her at the Cairo Airport.

"What... what's this?" she asked.

"I traveled to Egypt hoping to cure my depression. While returning, I bought lots of chocolates from the airport. I also bought this ring. I was happy. I was hopeful. I still believed you would come back.

"It's hilarious that while I was buying the ring, you were about four months pregnant with your second child." I continued. "I wanted to meet you and put the ring on your finger. And then you told me that I shouldn't have sent the chocolates. That we weren't together anymore. When I asked if you were serious, you didn't even open the message. I wanted to give a beautiful ring as a token of my love to someone who wasn't even interested in opening my messages.

"You then messaged me five months later. Your entitled ass begged for Rs. 3500 right away. Holy shit! You really think you're something, huh? Have you no shame? After ignoring my message and making me feel like shit, you come back five months later and start making demands? I'm not kidding when I say that you have got to be the most shameless person I've ever come across.

"I needed it urgently. I was in dire need of money," she replied.

I ignored her message and continued, "And then, you asked how long will I cling to the past. I couldn't help but smile. Smile at your complete disregard of what you put me through. I swear... I feel like every time you've been slapped at home, you must have deserved it. I genuinely do.

"I had decided right there and then that I would treat you based on the kind of person you are and the way you treated me. That's the reason I treated you like shit during our final conversation. I wanted you to feel the pain and embarrassment that you inflicted on me for months on end.

"That didn't sit well with you. You once told me that you were raised like a princess. And you were speaking the absolute truth. You're used to belittling and treating other people like shit. You truly believe deep down inside that everyone's beneath you. And you got riled up when I treated you like the scum of the earth that you are.

"I knew that would be our last conversation. You were aware at that point that I wasn't going to give you a single penny. You had hoped that I'd act like a clown and send the money immediately out of love. I didn't. You had no use of me now. There was no need for you to keep talking to me after that. You found someone else to do your bidding. The doctor, Atul. You aren't a good woman," I finally finished my rant.

"Who the hell are you to judge me?" Lieshaa replied angrily. I had struck a nerve. The fact that she was raging was quite satisfying. She was usually calm, composed, and willfully ignorant of the damage she had done.

"Oh, but we're birds of the same feather. We're both evil. There was a time when I wasn't. I still don't know how I went from rejecting you to falling madly in love with you. But yeah, we're both pieces of shit for betraying Rahul. We're kinda the same when it comes to character, Lieshaa. And that's exactly why I can judge you. I know what you are, deep down inside. No one knows you better than me. I've seen the real you. The "you" on the inside. And she's ugly as hell."

She went offline. She had always been one to run away from the truth, from taking accountability.

Lieshaa sent another text the next evening.

"Can I ask you something? How's your family?”

"Your attempts to feign concern are laughably bad," I replied. "I wish you had shown this concern last year, instead of treating me like a disposable object."

There was no point in having a conversation with her anymore. There was no way her massive ego would allow her to take accountability for her actions. Before ending the conversation, I decided to make her realize the extent of her hypocrisy, her dishonesty, her evilness. I finally sent her screenshots of a bunch of messages that she had sent me over the years. This was the final one:

"I love you so much.. I can't live without you.. My dear mom… I swear on you. I love Abhilash so much... you're my god as well... please make my wish come true... please make sure Abhilash and I are together forever.. I love you n miss u..."

"Lieshaa, you didn't even spare your mom who isn't around anymore. After getting rejected, you used her to convince me your love was genuine, and I walked right into your trap. This is who you are. The kind of woman who can stoop to the deepest pits of hell to get what she wants. The absolute scum of the earth," I wrote.

This was the last straw. She wasn't brave enough to face the ugly truth.

She had blocked me. For life.

The time had finally come.

I was going to tell Rahul everything that had happened behind his back. Between two people he trusted the most.

But I was scared.

I was scared out of my wits. I could only imagine what he would do once he found out about us. And it was terrifying.

Days turned into weeks. Weeks turned into months. In early February, I finally decided that it was now or never. I had to do it.

That night, I lay down on the bed and began typing a message on my phone. My entire body was shaking with fear. I was sweating excessively. I had never been this scared.

A Broken Man

My name is Rahul. I just found out that my wife and my friend of 11 years had an affair behind my back.

I'm completely broken inside.

It was a quiet, peaceful night. I had just finished dinner. I received a message from Abhilash, my "friend."

"I need to tell you something. It's important," he wrote.

"Yeah, tell me. What's the matter," I curiously asked.

"Any chance you and Lieshaa could come over here? It would be better if I tell it to you in person. Need both of you to hear it."

"That won't be possible. I'm loaded with work at the moment. What happened? Just tell me here itself," I responded. I sensed right away that something wasn't right.

"Yeah. Wait," he wrote.

He sent another message a few minutes later.

The message that broke me.

"Lieshaa and I... we had an affair. She wrote her number in one of my books that you used to take home for her to read. I didn't open the book for the next five years. Six years ago, she found me on Facebook and we began talking. She later confessed that she had been in love with me since 2013 when she first saw me. I initially rejected her but caved in a few weeks later.

"I left my job to be close to her upon her request. I was lying when I said that I left the job after almost being attacked by an angry customer. She asked me to have a kid with her that she could raise with you. She also asked me to take her with me somewhere far away and marry her. I said no to all of those things, but eventually said yes. We met at my home multiple times. We met outside as well. We finally broke up in March 2022 when she dumped me," he wrote. He then sent me several pictures that he and my wife used to click during their meetings. He also sent me a document containing screengrabs of the texts that he and my wife had exchanged over the years.

I glanced through the document over the next few minutes. I looked at pictures of him and my wife. Together. Happy. In love. I kept looking at the pictures for almost a minute. I could swear, though, that every single second felt like an eternity. It was as if time had stopped.

"My second daughter... is she yours? Please tell me the truth," I asked him.

"She's not mine. She did ask me to put a baby in her. But I rejected her proposal. By the time I was ready, she had moved on and had another daughter with you. She probably has had other affairs, so I'm not entirely sure. She told me that she was in love with a doctor. If she was at home in March-April 2022, the daughter is yours."

"No, she didn't go out if I remember correctly. But I will have to do a DNA test. I need to know," I replied. I couldn't stop shaking. "All girls are the same. My wife is a characterless, heartless woman. But you... I trusted you."

"I'm at home. You can come anytime you want. I'm ready for the consequences," he wrote.

"I can't. I won't. I won't be able to face the man who... I still can't believe that the two people... I'm short of words. I wish we had never met," I responded. "She had a child with me when you and her... all she had to do was tell me she didn't want to be with me and I would have gladly given her a divorce. I always knew what kind of a woman she was. If only I knew about this affair, I would've divorced her for sure. Tell me something... how many times did you two sleep with each other?"

"We met several times at my home..."

"When was the last time the two of you did it?"

"Late 2021."

"Think twice. Are you sure it wasn't sometime around April 2022? It doesn't matter anyway 'cause I'm divorcing her no matter what the test results are."

"No, I'm 100% sure."

"Why didn't you say anything before we had another daughter? I wouldn't have had another child with that cheating PoS if I knew about this."

"That's a question I'll keep asking myself till my very last breath," he answered.

I couldn't sleep that night. She was right beside me, sleeping like a baby, having no idea that I knew everything. I was devastated. I kept looking at the pictures all night. While I was out there working, she used to go and meet him, hold him, and make love to him. Then, she would return, look me in the eye, and smile, pretending to be mine.

It was 4 already. I couldn't hold back my tears. I was repeatedly wiping them off while looking at how happy and content she looked with him in those pictures.

In the morning, I decided to confront her. I couldn't live this lie anymore.

"Lieshaa... I have something to show you," I said while handing my phone over to her.

The color drained from her face as soon as she looked at the screen. She stood right there, not moving an inch. She kept looking at the screen as tears started running down her face.

"I... these must be fake, photoshopped. I have no idea about any of these. These are edited pictures," she said, crying loudly.

I kept looking at her. With no emotion on my face.

There's a saying. If a woman lies to you, it means she doesn't respect you one bit. She thinks that you are naive and stupid enough to believe her lies. You're nothing more than a clown to her.

My wife, the "love of my life," was telling me with a straight face that those pictures were edited, photoshopped. I was putting every bit of my energy into controlling my rage.

It was the longest day of my 38-year life.

It didn't take long for her to finally admit that the pictures were real. She met him. She made love to him. She cheated on me with him. For four years.

"Please... I beg you, I swear on my mom, my dad... I don't love him. I never loved him. That bastard... he... he was the one who forced me to meet him and sleep with him. I always told him no, but he kept forcing me... please believe me," she said. Her eyes were blood-red at this point. It had been about three hours since she saw the pictures and she still hadn't stopped crying.

"I thought you loved me. I am such an idiot for believing you again. You're the same woman you were before we got married," I said in a defeated tone.

"I do. I always did. I always loved you. Why would I have another daughter with you if I didn't love you? Please... believe me on this!"

"I've read the messages. You literally asked him to give you a baby, a request that he rejected," I said, waiting eagerly for her response.

She had none.

An hour later, she came towards me and began pleading with me again.

"He's the biggest loser I've ever seen. He has no class, no shame, no respect for women, he's always treated me like shit," she said. "I had been wanting to leave him from the very beginning but he kept pressuring me into staying with him. Please believe me. We… we need to file a case against him."

I stayed silent.

She then got on her knees, held my feet with both of her hands, and started begging me to forgive her. She was crying uncontrollably and asking me for forgiveness. She vowed to never cheat on me again.

I had read her chats with Abhilash. Starting from 2018, all the way to the end. She had told countless lies today in a desperate attempt to get me to forgive her.

She used to call him her husband, told him that he meant more to her than me, swore on her dead mom that she would never leave him, pleaded with him to give her a baby, and even asked him to take her away from me.

And now, this woman was calling him the biggest loser she had ever seen. The evil witch was ready to file a case against him just to convince me that she loved me.

But if that happened, their chats and pictures would become public, everyone would know of their affair, and people would become aware of how exactly it all started. How she wrote her number in his book, found him on Facebook years later, spent weeks on end convincing him to accept her proposal, and begged him to marry her.

I then realized something. And it broke me even more.

For years, she told him that she loved him. No one forced her to do so. Her feelings for him were real. On the other hand, she told me she loved me ONLY WHEN I found out about her affair and was planning to give her a divorce. Her feelings for me were far from real.

She was an incredibly dangerous woman, ready to throw anyone to the wolves if it meant she would be safe.

But I had no choice but to stay with her. We had two children together.

If he had told me the truth before we had another child, I would've divorced her right there and taken our daughter with me.

But it was too late now. This woman... this vile woman. I used to fight with my parents for her, always took her side and married her despite their protests.

And she cheats on me with my friend.

I messaged Abhilash that night.

"Forget her. After I leave her, she will come crawling to you, ask for your forgiveness, and convince you to marry her. A few months down the line, she will cheat on you as well, the way she cheated on me with you. I know that woman since we were teenagers," I wrote.

"So... what will she do if you leave her?" Abhilash asked.

"This," I responded and sent a picture. A picture of me, Lieshaa, and our two kids. "No one's leaving anyone, Abhilash."

"Oh, I feared this would happen. That woman has something in her. Her tears... they have this power that can melt the hardest rocks. She's used them against me in the past. This isn't surprising in the least."

"Abhilash, you need to forget her. For good. I haven't forgiven her. And I never will. She slept with my friend behind my back. But she has two kids with me. I wish you had told me the truth two years ago before we planned our second child. But what's done is done. MOVE ON."

"Listen, that woman has wasted five years of my life. FIVE YEARS. A person has a lifespan of about 70 years and I wasted five of mine on that wretched scum of the earth. I'll never forget her, and I'll never forgive her. There's still a part of me that loves her. The part that keeps recalling every single lie she told. Every single promise she broke. Those beautiful lies of hers are going to stay with me till the very end," he wrote.

"If you loved her so much, why didn't you take her away like you had planned?" I asked.

"I was going to. DAMMIT! I had been planning to fulfill her wish since late 2018. Every single penny I earned was going to go towards our future. Together. Away from you. Just like she wanted. Like I wanted. I guess she lost interest somewhere in the middle. Most probably during the pandemic. But what I will never understand is that even after COVID died down, she kept promising me that she loved me and asked me to take her away from you. She kept saying this till the end, before suddenly dumping me."

"Well, there's no use crying over spilled milk now. Find someone. Someone with a good character, who's kind-hearted and isn't faking it. And marry her. Forget about Lieshaa," I replied.

"That won't happen. I know I'll never see her again, but I can't forget her. No chance in hell. It's not easy forgetting someone who promised you the world, spent four years hyping up a beautiful future that was never going to come, and then left you crying, confused, hateful. I'll never be able to move on. I'll never forget her. You take care of her, Rahul."

"Haha!" I wrote, a smile forming on my face. "I've always taken care of her."

"Then why did she come to me?" he asked.

I was done responding.

"Lieshaa... such a pretty name. Such a pretty face. The prettiest I've ever seen, or will ever see. Those messages of hers... that sweet, comforting voice. There are times when I forget that she will never talk to me again. It's hard to fathom that someone who couldn't go a day without talking to me, will spend the rest of her life happily, without ever uttering a word to me.

"This isn't what she had told me. This isn't what she had promised. This woman... this wicked, cold-hearted monster... this isn't Lieshaa. At least not the one who once told me that she would never stop loving me. Why did she come into my life, loved me like no one else ever did, and then left me all of a sudden? I'll keep wondering that till my very last breath," he wrote, before going offline.

A Mistake

I just had what was possibly my final conversation with Rahul.

He had forgiven Lieshaa.

He had no other choice. He also told me everything that had happened between the two of them. The things she said about me. Horrible, appalling things. She had called me a loser. After spending years on end badmouthing Rahul to convince me that she was mine, she had now changed her tune to make him forgive her. A few months after telling me that she was planning on filing a case against her husband, she told him that she wanted to file one against me. At that moment, I breathed a sigh of relief, knowing that I didn't delete any of her messages. After I was done chatting with him, I blocked him everywhere.

I then checked Lieshaa's WhatsApp profile. The profile photo had been changed. Mere hours ago. For the first time in six years, the profile picture featured the husband-wife duo.

Rahul was looking at the camera with Lieshaa standing behind him. She had her hands gently placed on his right shoulder. I could sense the hatred oozing out of those brown, dry eyes. Her face looked like she had been crying the whole day. It was clear as day that the picture was taken shortly after he "forgave" her. The woman who never bothered to put her husband in her profile picture was now proudly posing with him.

She wanted me to see it. She wanted me to know that she had been forgiven. She wanted me to stay out of her life.

For four years, we were inseparable. She wanted no one else but me. She used to spend hours badmouthing Rahul. She was ready to leave what she described as a miserable life and start a new one with me. And now, she was looking at me through my phone's screen, posing with the same man she once hated with all her heart. Back in 2018, I would've never imagined that she would be putting up a profile picture with him with the sole purpose of letting me know that I needed to fuck off.

After coming into my life UNINVITED, coercing me into reciprocating her love by swearing on her dead mom, stringing me along for four long years, and suddenly throwing it all away, she wanted me to suck it up and move on.

Deep down inside, all I wanted was for karma to catch up to her someday and make her feel the same pain that I felt because of her actions.

I needed to move on. It was over.

But there was one last thing left to do.

February 8, 2024, 11:00 a.m.

This strange, unreal life of mine.

On February 8, 2009, I skipped my maths viva, losing 20 precious internal marks in the process. It led to me failing 12th grade in what was the worst moment of my life back then.

But it also led to Lieshaa coming into my life. She showered all the love in the world upon me for years, before suddenly leaving me alone. And now, on February 8, we were going to come face-to-face one last time.

I had been contemplating this for the past few days.

I wanted to have one last conversation with Lieshaa. I couldn't move on without confronting her one last time. I finished my work early. After putting on a T-shirt and jeans, I headed out of the house and began walking. I didn't even bother taking the bike. It was as if I was in a trance.

I passed by the house at the end of the block, before which she once stood while Rahul was getting books for her.

I passed by the grocery shop where I once bought two chocolate bars for her before meeting her for the first time.

I passed by my old apartment, which was a five-minute walk away from her home.

I passed by the tuition class I used to attend in '05, which was right beside her home.

I then passed by her home, and Rahul's was now visible in the distance.

I stopped in my tracks. A part of me was deathly afraid of what could happen in the next few minutes. I stood in the same spot for a while and contemplated letting it go, turning back, and heading home.

It just didn't feel right, though. I had to let her know what I thought of her. I had to make her aware of the damage she had caused. I had to remind her of the promises she once made. I had to expose every single lie that she had told me over the course of four years.

I had to let her know that she was the most evil woman I had ever seen.

I wanted to make sure she remembered what she had done every time she looked in the mirror. It was highly unlikely, though. She had proven time and again that she could ruin someone's life and sleep like a baby that very night, without a shred of remorse in her heart.

I was determined. I had prepared myself for the worst if it meant that I would get to confront her. I had no idea what Rahul was going to do.

I started walking towards his home. A corner of the living room was visible from outside the gate. I took a deep breath and called out his name a couple of times. Seconds later, he appeared at the door, a smile forming on his face as soon as he saw me.

"Abhilash! Come, come inside!" he exclaimed while opening the gate. He kept smiling, masking the awkwardness and tension between us.

His puppy came out of nowhere, pounced on me, and began licking my jeans. Rahul asked me to take a chair before tying the puppy up. He then picked up his 13-month-old toddler from the living room and took her inside. This was the first time that I had seen her, and it most certainly was going to be the last. Their older daughter hadn't returned from school yet.

Lieshaa was nowhere to be seen.

"How are you?" He asked. "What happened? Did you come on foot?"

He was doing his absolute best to make me feel comfortable. His unexpectedly nice behavior unnerved me to no end, though.

What's the only thing scarier than a dangerous man who knows you've wronged him?

A dangerous man who knows you've wronged him… smiling at you.

I hadn't forgotten what a classmate had told me about him back when we were pursuing engineering.

"He once went into a guy's home and beat him up just for staring at her a couple of times."

And here I was, sitting right in front of him, days after revealing to him that Lieshaa and I had been having an affair behind his back for four years. My hatred for the woman who had ruined my life had brought me here, and I was scared that the worst was about to happen at any moment.

"I... I wanted to talk to Liesh... Lieshaa, one last time," I said, hesitatingly.

"NO," a loud voice came from the adjacent room. It was her. It wasn't surprising that the most evil woman I had ever met was a gutless coward as well. The last thing she wanted was to face me. To face the ghost from her past. To face the man she once claimed was her one true love.

To face the ugly truth behind the countless lies she had told me.

"Lieshaa, just talk it out with him for a while and give him closure," Rahul said.

"No," she said bluntly, again.

"Why did you have an affair with him then? Why did you make him promises you couldn't keep?" he asked her.

"I made a mistake... it was a mistake," she shouted at the top of her lungs.

A mistake.

A MISTAKE.

"Abhi, I love your eyes, your hair, your lips... what I'm trying to say is that you're perfect!"

A mistake.

I love you so much... I can't live without you..."

A mistake.

"My dear mom, I love Abhilash so much!"

A mistake.

"I've never loved someone as much as you. Not even Rahul. Believe me!"

A mistake.

"I want to marry you. I want a baby from you, a mini version of you."

A mistake.

"I love you with all my heart and will continue to do so for the rest of my life, Abhi."

A mistake.

Nine years. Innumerable promises. Those warm hugs. Those soft, tender kisses of hers. The way her eyes used to gleam while looking into mine.

A mistake. All of it... a mistake.

A life ruined.

A heart broken into pieces.

A man betrayed.

His dreams crushed.

For this wretched woman, it was a mistake.

I broke down. Right in front of Rahul. He handed me a glass of water and began patting me on the back. A few moments later, I collected myself and wiped the tears off my face.

"After destroying my life beyond repair, you have the gall to say that it was all a mistake? I'm not leaving. I can't leave without having a conversation with you," I said, facing the room. "I'm sorry, but after what you've put me through, the least you can do is face me and listen to what I have to say."

"NO!" she didn't budge.

I didn't budge as well. She knew I was not going to leave unless she listened to me.

A few seconds later, she appeared at the door. Rahul left to tend to the baby in the other room. He had sensed that I wouldn't be able to talk freely with him sitting right in front of me.

"Sit," I said.

She hesitated, her eyes pinned to the floor. I didn't say a word. She finally took a seat on the couch, a few feet away from me.

"Look at me while I'm talking to you."

She looked at me for a fraction of a second before quickly bowing her head down. She was embarrassed. Embarrassed of facing the man she had put through hell. It was better to begin the conversation instead of wasting more time.

"Why?"

"I can't. I have a family. I can't leave them for you. I simply can't. I'm sorry," she said and began sobbing. "Rahul is suspicious of me... wants to take a DNA test even though he's the father."

"You mean, actions have consequences? What a strange concept, huh? You're way smarter than I had ever imagined, the way you're trying to pretend that you're a victim here. And what about the things you said, the promises you made, the future you made me wait for? For four years! You had a family back then as well, didn't you? Why did you come after me, then? WHY?"

Utter silence.

"I need to say something," she finally broke the silence.

"What?" I asked.

"First of all, I never once came to meet you. It was never my choice. You were the only one who wanted to meet me and form a physical relationship with me. Also, I cut off all contact with you sometime around March. It's been a long time since we even talked with each other."

I was horrified.

I was disgusted.

At that moment, it took every bit of strength and willpower that I had to contain my rage.

This woman... she knew I had the messages. She knew Rahul had seen them. And yet, she chose to lie to my face.

I looked at her dead in the eyes. She still looked the same as the first time I had seen her.

But somehow, she had never looked uglier.

"Give me the past six years of my life back."

"Wh... what?" she looked at me in confusion.

"You fuc... YOU ABSOLUTE FUCKING MONSTER! You... you have two daughters. You are a mother. You're supposed to be nurturing, kind-hearted, loving. And yet I've never seen a bigger piece of shit than you. First of all, you DID talk to me on multiple occasions after March 2022. You assured me that we were still in love. You told me that you would love to have a baby with me. You begged me for money like the shameless tramp that you are, AFTER ignoring me for about five months. Why resort to lying when I have EVERY SINGLE text of yours saved, you absolute fucking scumbag?"

I took a deep breath. Six years ago, I quit my job for this evil witch just 'cause she wanted me to be closer to her. And now, she was telling me that I was the one who forced her to meet me and sleep with me.

"Listen... you once told me that Rahul went into a guy's home and beat him up for trying to pursue you. Let me drop some truth bombs on you. He doesn't hold a candle to you when it comes to hurting someone. The wounds that guy suffered from Rahul's beating must've healed in a few days, two weeks max. But the things you did, you self-righteous woman, gave me two of the darkest years of my life and drove me to the point of almost taking my own life. The wounds you gave me are here to stay till the last breath of my life. The tears in your eyes and the lies coming out of your mouth are WAYYYY deadlier than the worst beatings Rahul has ever inflicted on guys who stared at you.

"I wonder how gloriously fucked I would have been if I hadn't saved our chats. I have about 250 different messages that you've sent over the years, in which you've begged me to meet you, where you've pleaded with me to make love to you in the wildest ways imaginable. I've already sent our chats to Rahul, but I'll read a few of them out right in front of you. Remember, you brought this upon yourself. All I wanted was closure. I didn't want to do this. You made me do it," I said, as calmly as I could.

I took out my phone and began reading the texts aloud.

"You'll never stop meeting me, right?"

"We're meeting this weekend... I can't... live without you."

"Abhilash... we'll meet, right? Wanna see you. Especially your eyes."

"Meet me now, please. NOW."

"Meet me... in a few days. I want to meet you."

"And it goes on and on and on..." I said while putting the phone back in my pocket.

Again, I've come for closure, not to fight with you or to hear more of your lies. You've lied enough to last a lifetime, Liesh. So, listen. Don't speak, unless you have something to say that isn't a lie."

She didn't say a word.

I had waited for this moment for two long years. I finally had the chance to tell her everything. To pour my heart out. To say all the things that had been running in my mind since March 2022.

"2013 was hands down the worst year of my life. Rahul and Samay had stopped attending classes after failing the previous year and I was alone. Every day felt like a drag, I was depressed, didn't talk much, and kept to myself. Years later, I met you and realized that 2013 was far from the worst year of my life. In fact, it was THE BEST. You loved me back then. You cared for me back then. You were yearning to see me, meet me, hold me back then. It didn't matter that I didn't have any idea about your feelings. What mattered was when I was alone, depressed, and felt like shit, someone was out there, who gave a damn about me.

"And now, I can't help but cry my eyes out knowing that the woman who loved me like crazy back then would now prefer seeing me drop dead," I said, while looking at her, tears running down my cheeks. "It's heartbreaking to realize that the woman of my dreams, the sweetest person I had ever met, is a cheap, treacherous roadside tramp at best. I have lost the ability to be happy. No matter what, I just can't feel true happiness anymore. I haven't felt it since March 14, TWO YEARS AGO. I still find it hard to believe that I was stupid enough to get betrayed by a lowlife scum like you. What did you take me for, anyway? A guy you would have some fun with and dump him when you're done quenching your lust? I'm much, much more than that, you evil witch!

"You once told me that a friend of yours was aware that you were in love with me back in 2013. You said that she told you to quit trying to pursue me because I probably wouldn't have reciprocated your feelings. Lieshaa, was this really what your friend said? Or did she say something like, 'Enough! You're married to Rahul and are already having a couple of affairs behind his back. Don't add another one and complicate things!' Now that I know the real you, there's a high possibility that this was what she told you.

"I still sometimes find it hard to fathom that an objectively evil woman like you is the mother of two little kids. Your cold, dead heart will never realize what I go through every day, knowing that you're most certainly talking to other guys now. It's in your blood. It's in your character. You simply can't help it. You need to have new, fresh faces to quench your lust every few months. The guy whose text you once saved in the Notes app… that doctor, Atul…

"I sometimes picture you lying on your bed at night, chatting with a new guy, making promises to him, assuring that you love him more than anyone else, more than Rahul. You even swear on your dead mom, like you did with me years ago. You have a smile on your face while you're doing so, having already forgotten that you said the same things to me for years before throwing me away. That pain... I wish you could feel it at least for a split second. I'm quite sure you ignored someone else back in 2018 when you met me. Someone you got bored of. I've taken his spot now. And the guy, or guys you're speaking with now, secretly behind Rahul's back, will take my spot someday. This vicious cycle of yours... you're an utterly horrible and awful human being, Lieshaa."

She was dead silent. Her eyes hadn't moved one bit and were still pinned to the floor.

"My life was going pretty well. I had a job to look forward to. A whole life to look forward to. I wanted to make my parents happy. And then you came into my life. You did everything to make me love you back but to no avail. I eventually fell in love with you AFTER BELIEVING YOUR LIES and left my freaking job just to be near you! Why wouldn't I believe you? You swore on your dead mom that you loved me. And it turned out to be a lie. WHO DOES THAT? HOW DEPRAVED ONE HAS TO BE TO DO THAT?

"And then you told me about the number in the book. And I finally fell in love with you. Five years. You had waited five years. It made me believe we were destined to be together. You showered me with love and emotional support when my mom was in the hospital, battling jaundice. You played well, 'cause that was one of the reasons why I eventually fell for you. You made me believe that you genuinely cared about every aspect of my life, including my loved ones. I wasted four fucking years of my life on you and didn't even look at another woman. I wish I had two-timed you, played with your emotions, used you the way you used me, and cheated on you when I had the chance. You're someone who DESERVES to be cheated on and I'll forever regret believing you and rejecting advances from other women.

"Talking to you was something I used to look forward to every night. You'll never understand how much it meant to me. And you took it away from me. My blood pressure... I used to fear that I would suddenly drop dead one day, and you wouldn't even know about it until a few days after my passing. And even after you learned of my death, you wouldn't give a damn 'cause I'm of no use to you now. All those promises of yours, the dreams we saw together, just for it to end in such a manner. It hurts more than your stone-cold heart can ever fathom. Every single moment I've spent with you... that smile of yours behind the college, watching you as you stood near my home as Rahul was taking books from me, picking you up on my bike six years later, and every single time we met over the next four years... I'll keep rewinding those moments till the very end of my life," I said.

"Four years into our relationship, I realized that I would gladly give my life for you. People don't do that for their flesh and blood, Liesh... but I loved you to the extent that I was ready to do anything for you. I bought a freaking ring for you in Egypt while you were here, knowing full well that you wanted nothing to do with me. And then, you ended it like I meant nothing to you. Here's what I think. You probably thought that this wouldn't last long, right? You thought that you would have some fun, and so will I. We will have an affair behind his back and then go our separate ways, right? Except, you made me innumerable promises of eternal love. You didn't even spare your mom while making those promises."

"I'm sorry. I... I jus--"

"Shhh! Your apologies mean ABSOLUTELY NOTHING. Based on the way you've treated me over the past two years, both you and I know that your apologies don't mean shit. I'm here for closure, let me get it. Just... stay silent and let me get it," I requested her.

I continued, "Between 2014-2018, I never once thought of you. Didn't even know your name. I miss not knowing anything about you. Now, not a day goes by without me thinking about you. And it hurts like hell, realizing you aren't mine anymore. I've become a hateful person over the past two years. I have started hating women. I'm basically an incel now. I find it hard to trust people, to treat them well, to make new friends, to love someone. Your betrayal has turned my life upside down. My simple mind still finds it hard to comprehend how you wake up every day, talk to your kids, eat food, watch TV, and hang out with friends, knowing full well that your actions have destroyed a person from within, and he's out there, depressed and alone. You're truly a monster in the garb of an innocent, loving, caring woman.

"What breaks my heart the most is the fact that I'll never get to see your old, caring, loving self again, even if it was a mask that was hiding your true face. I'll never receive a text or a call from you, something I used to look forward to every night. Even if you reach out someday, I won't forget the pain you caused me over the past two years. It hurts knowing that you are absolute trash in my eyes now and I will always miss that side of yours that you faked while trying to make me yours. Sometimes at night, I start wondering why you still haven't messaged. And then reality hits. I end up breaking down into tears, realizing that I will never receive another text from you again. You absolute filth, you heartless piece of shit."

She gaped at me with shocked eyes but didn't say a word. Her entitled self couldn't fathom that I was throwing profanities at her for ruining my life.

"You had promised me eternal love. Now, all you have towards me is hate. Why the fuck would you hate me for believing you and wanting you to keep your promise? I should be the one who has the right to hate you! You had your fun and then one day, you went, 'Oops! I'm done, but he's still into me! What do I do now? Well, I'll just leave him out of the blue and not bother anymore.' Our story was supposed to end with us living happily ever after like you had promised. And now, it's going to end with me leaving this world someday, full of regret and hatred. I don't know why your betrayal surprised me when I was aware that you had been cheating on him with me for years. I guess the fact that you swore on your dead mom made me believe your lies."

I had been rambling for the past 10 minutes. I took a sip of water before resuming my rant.

"The red flags were right in front of me. You cheated on Rahul with me and I was dumb enough to believe that I was special. When a person truly loves someone, they ignore every red flag, like I did. I saved every message of yours so that we could read them together someday after getting married. I didn't have the slightest idea that those messages were going to save me from your lying ass. You were ready to file a case against me, you... you..." I broke down.

"I tried dating other women, I did. I genuinely wanted to leave your memories behind and move on. But I just couldn't. I couldn't forget the promises you made to me. I still can't believe that this empty shell of a human being who's devoid of any emotion, once made me fall in love with her and swore that we would never part.

"Last year, you blocked me after I showed you the message where you had pleaded with your dead mom to keep us together forever. Do you know why you blocked me? At that moment, you realized the extent of your evilness and were ashamed of the fact that you used your dead mom to trap a guy. The guilt set in, and you were unable to handle the truth. As you always have done, you took the easy path and blocked me.

"Also, you called me a loser. Yeah, he told me. Listen, you scum of the earth! I didn't even know you. You used to come to the college with Rahul in hopes that I would notice you and fall in love with you. I didn't look at you even once back then. You didn't mean anything to me. Your desperate ass came running to me five years later, begging me to make you mine. When I rejected you, you swore on your dead mom that you truly loved me, and that was when I fell into your trap. Again, I didn't even know you. And all these years later, you're calling me a loser? Why? Just because I expected you to keep the promise that you made while swearing on your mom? I'm sure she's looking down on you at this very moment and there's nothing but shame and regret in her heart.

"My mom, she took great pains over the past thirty years to raise me right. Years of hard work, nurturing, waking up every day at five, sending me to school, seeing me succeed in academics, and dreaming about a better future for me. I can't help but recall struggling in school, failing 12th grade, getting back up, studying hard for the next six years, going through tough and rigorous college schedules and exams one after the other and never failing again. All of that, only to have my life ruined by an incredibly dumb skank who wouldn't have survived even a semester in engineering? All of that, just for a two-bit tramp to come into my life, ruin it forever, and then call me a loser? I want you to know this... if you really want to see the biggest loser, look no further than in the mirror. I want to let you know that you don't have the slightest idea how much pain and anguish you've caused me and my loved ones.

"The fact that you've destroyed me beyond repair and have absolutely no remorse speaks volumes about the kind of human you are and the kind of upbringing you have had. I mean, who the fuck are you at this point? You used to be caring, kind, and every inch of your being had nothing but love towards me. Now, you've turned into this vile, heartless woman who doesn't give a shit about me and that honestly breaks my heart! How the hell can you look in the mirror every day, you disgusting excuse of a woman? Don't you feel even the tiniest bit of shame realizing that you used your dead mom to trap me?" I was fuming with anger at this point.

I could see that she was angry as well.

She probably wanted to talk back, but feared that I'd take out my phone again and bring up one of her countless lies.

"Another thing. I know evil minds don't work the way normal ones do. They never take accountability and never believe that they're at fault. You're probably thinking, 'Why did he come into my life?' Instead, I want you to ask yourself the following: 'Why did I come into his life, make false promises, destroy him, and leave him a broken man?' Lieshaa, I know you hate me. I want you to know that I hate you with all my heart as well. And unlike you, I have a reason to hate you. You once promised me that our love would last till our final breaths. Obviously, you were lying through your teeth. But I'm not. I promise you, my hatred and disdain for you will last till my final breath.

"I also need you to know that you aren't capable of truly loving someone. You were once ready to leave your husband and daughter for me. After promising me the world for years on end, you eventually got bored of me and decided to casually end it one day. The way you treated me after dumping me... I won't ever forget it. If the right opportunity arises, you will drop everything you hold dear and try to grab it. You aren't capable of forming genuine, loving relationships. You aren't a woman who can be loved and cherished. You're the kind of person who's only good for a one-night stand, or maybe a bunch of hookups. If a guy ever tries to fall in love with your two-timing ass, he's bound to suffer the same fate that Rahul and I did.

"I truly believe that if we had gone ahead with our plan to run away and get married, I would have suffered the same fate as Rahul. You definitely would've cheated on me with someone else, maybe one of my friends. I'm kinda glad it didn't come to that. We had our fun, and I'll now try to find someone to spend the rest of my life with. Every guy needs a Lieshaa in his life to have some fun with before he meets an actual good woman he can have a kid with. You're not the kind of woman a guy would want to marry. Rahul did and is regretting it now. What hurts is the fact that I know you're nothing special, and yet I fell into the trap of an ordinary woman like you. I really, really believed you were one of a kind, but you aren't. You're one of the most basic women I've ever seen. There's like a billion women like you out there. I got my life ruined by someone like you when I could've spent that time finding a good woman."

The pure rage in her eyes... I was reveling in it.

"Hey, back in mid-2022, while I was suffering from severe depression after your betrayal, you once yelled at me and told me that I was destroying your family. You had grown tired of my texts and calls. Remember this... back in 2018, when you were trying to woo me, your never-ending messages used to get on my nerves sometimes. I never yelled at you or asked you to stop. I always respected the fact that you thought highly of me, no matter how annoying your messages were getting. Remember, we're not the same.

"My mom must've cried for me a million times over the past two years. No woman wants to see her son suffer. You need to understand that you did this. You ruined a man to such a degree that his mom could do nothing but cry herself to sleep every night. You did this. You, a mother of two daughters. How would you feel if someone played with your daughters' lives the way you played with the life of someone's son? Your evil mind can't even comprehend the pain you've inflicted on me and my family. You've taught me a lesson that the greatest of teachers never could."

I needed to get away from her. I couldn't look at her anymore.

"I think about you all the time. When I order pizza from the food truck I once told you about, when it rains, when I look at the book that still has your number written on it, when I drive on the roads we once used to drive on, when I see happy couples in love... I can't seem to forget you, and probably never will. From the bottom of my heart, I hope you never suffer the way you made me suffer. Believe me, you wouldn't last a minute. And yeah, you said it was all a mistake, right? Liesh... using someone to satisfy your sexual desires, making promises you never intend to keep, and throwing them away after getting bored... that isn't a mistake. You know what a mistake is?"

She looked at me.

The incessant crying had messed up her face almost beyond recognition. I got up from the chair and approached her.

"Believing your lies, now that was a mistake. One which I'll regret till I take my last breath," I whispered into her ear.

Rahul came outside moments later and sat on the couch. I began walking towards the door before stopping a few feet away from it.

"Oh! One last thing," I said, while staring at her.

"I LOVE YOU SO MUCH.. I CAN'T LIVE WITHOUT YOU.. MY DEAR MOM... I SWEAR ON YOU. I LOVE ABHILASH SO MUCH... YOU'RE MY GOD AS WELL... PLEASE MAKE MY WISH COME TRUE... PLEASE MAKE SURE ABHILASH AND I ARE TOGETHER FOREVER.. I LOVE YOU N MISS U..."

I read her message aloud on my phone while keeping my eyes locked with hers.

She kept mum. I didn't say another word. There was no need.

She was aware of what she had done. Aware that she had used her mother to emotionally manipulate a guy into reciprocating her love. Aware that her words, her promises, and her lies would flash in front of her eyes every single time she looked in the mirror for the rest of her life.

I took one last look at her, with the events of the past decade or so flashing before my eyes in a matter of seconds. Right from the day she smiled at me while we came across each other behind the college, all the way to this very moment.

The next minute, I was outside her home. I then began walking away. While making a turn at the corner, I felt as if I was turning the last page of a book that had taken me 11 years to finish.

I never saw Lieshaa again.

"I betrayed your trust, and yet you let me in and allowed me to speak to Lieshaa one last time. I won't ask for forgiveness 'cause I honestly don't deserve it, but I'm sorry for everything. I'm truly sorry," I sent Rahul a text after coming back home.

That evening, he sent me a text.

"Did you block me?"

I didn't respond.

"Can you unblock me, it's important," he sent another text.

I unblocked him from WhatsApp and other platforms before sending him a message.

"I'm sorry. I had to block you everywhere. I don't want to see her face ever again and feared you might put up a picture with her on social media somewhere down the line. I've blocked her as well."

"The moment I learned about the affair, I removed all pictures of her. I'm never putting her picture again after what she's done," he replied. "Also, I'm coming over. Are you home?"

"Yeah, I am. What happened?" I asked.

"I just needed to talk for a while. I'll be there in a few minutes."

I quickly changed clothes and stepped out of the house. I headed to the garden at the end of the block. Except for one of my neighbors who was walking his dog, there was no one in the garden.

Rahul arrived after about 10 minutes and parked his moped outside the garden.

"Can we sit somewhere else? Like a bar or a restaurant?" He asked. "I just didn't feel like staying at home and wanted to get some fresh air. I haven't eaten as well."

"Yeah, sure. Let's go! There are a few places nearby," I didn't want to say no to anything he asked of me.

We hopped on his moped and headed outside the colony.

"I wanted to have a few drinks. I know you don't drink, and I haven't had a drink in almost two decades, but I seriously need a few tonight," he said.

I could sense the pain in his voice.

"Listen, alcohol will ruin things even more," I pleaded to him. "Please... once you start, you're bound to get addicted to it. Do one thing, stop in front of that bakery."

I quickly grabbed an energy drink and a chocolate shake from the bakery and hopped on the moped.

"Here, have this," I handed him the can of energy drink and began drinking the chocolate shake I had bought for myself.

"But I need to get a few drinks inside me, Abhilash," he said while gulping down the energy drink.

For the next five minutes or so, I did everything in my power to stop him from drinking again. He was hell-bent on having at least one drink, though. He was hurt and felt a few drinks would help him drown his sorrows.

"I would have gladly sat down with you in a bar and let you have a couple of drinks. But what would happen next? You have a daughter and a toddler at home. They've never seen you come home drunk. And what if you can't control your emotions? If you didn't have kids, I would have happily accompanied you to the bar. But you simply can't do this to them. What if it becomes a habit and you start drinking every day? I guarantee you, it's going to affect them in more ways than one," I said.

As soon as I mentioned his kids, Rahul realized that touching alcohol again was a terrible idea. He dropped the thought and didn't mention it again.

"Also, I haven't eaten. Have you?" he asked. I hadn't had dinner as well. I began searching for restaurants nearby. Shortly after, we were outside Al Zam Zam, the same restaurant where Rahul, Samay, and I went for dinner after completing our mini project, back in 2013.

11 years.

Back then, I didn't even know his wife's name. And then, the craziest, most unimaginable things happened over the next 11 years. And here we were, having dinner at the same restaurant again.

I once heard a saying, "Truth is stranger than fiction." I couldn't agree more.

After finishing the dinner, we headed back to my colony. Rahul mostly remained silent during dinner and I was anxious to hear what he had to say.

We entered the garden again and began walking.

"I've read those chats that you and Lieshaa had over five or so years. You told her today that you are going to move on, but it might not be as easy for you as you think. The reason I came to meet you is to tell you a few things that might help you move on and forget her forever."

Was Rahul concerned that I was never going to move on from Lieshaa and wanted to make sure I did? Or was he genuinely worried for my well-being and wanted me to turn my life around for the better?

I couldn't tell.

"Listen. She's ruined my life, but yours is still intact. You made an incredibly stupid mistake by leaving your government job for a woman like her. But you now have another job so it's all good. You need to find a good woman and get married. You believed every word she told you and here you are, full of regrets. Even though she threw you away after using you for her pleasure, you still seem to have a soft spot for her. I'm here to make you aware of the dark, ugly reality of your "perfect" love story with her," he said.

"You're not the only one she's had an affair with. You once believed her to be the most grounded, down-to-earth, soft-hearted, caring woman you had ever met. Obviously, she is far from that, and you've learned it the hard way, Abhilash.

"Lieshaa and I met way back in '06, seven years before she met you. I fell for her immediately and began pursuing her relentlessly. She finally said yes about two years later. I had never been happier, but my nightmare had just begun. It didn't take long for me to realize that she wasn't anywhere close to what she pretended to be. But I was madly in love. Looks can be deceiving, and it couldn't be truer in Lieshaa's case."

"What do you mean? What did she do?" I asked. My curiosity was at its peak.

"She was insanely pretty. Every other day, she used to tell me about guys in her college asking her out. I've beaten the hell out of three different guys who bothered her. The last one, I went inside his home to beat him up."

I knew he was telling the truth. Lieshaa had told me this story once.

"But the thing was, she LOVED the attention. She couldn't get enough of guys throwing themselves at her and giving her anything she desired. Someone once informed me that she was with a guy in an apartment. Minutes later, I was outside the apartment. And then I caught her. I won't go into the details of what happened next, but it was ugly."

I gaped at him in utter shock.

"On one occasion, I caught her getting intimate with a guy from her college at the annual gathering. Imagine how I must've felt, seeing her making out with another guy while she was in a relationship with me.

"I suspected her at all times and for good reason. There was one time when we were about to head to our respective homes after roaming around on my bike. After I dropped her near her home, I snatched her phone from her hand and rode away, while she kept yelling at me to stop. After I reached home, I checked her phone thoroughly and found tons of inappropriate messages exchanged between her and two different guys.

"On another occasion, I was roaming around with a friend on my bike. It was a Sunday. As we were passing by her college, my friend noticed that she was talking to a guy in a corner. He immediately told me and I stopped the bike. We sped towards them and stopped right in front of them. She was stunned, but quickly regained herself and began making excuses. "He's just a friend from my dance class," she said. I gave him a stern warning and told her to go home immediately. She didn't say a word and left on her moped," Rahul said.

"You... you still married her. Why?"

"Just like you, I loved her with all my heart. I couldn't imagine my life without her. I kept convincing myself that she would change after our wedding. But here we are. There's a possibility that she's on her phone right now, telling the same lies to someone else that she once told you and that she's been telling me for years."

I stopped in my tracks and broke down into tears.

I had bawled my eyes out for this woman. I had bought a ring for her. I had spent the past two years in severe depression because of her. I was about to end my life after she left me.

I thought she was special. One of a kind.

Lieshaa had me convinced that she was this loving, pure-hearted angel who could do no wrong. Every claim of hers turned out to be false but a part of me still believed that what she felt for me was genuine, at least in the beginning. The realization had hit me hard. She was a lowlife who desired every other guy she came across. The image of Lieshaa that was built in my heart was of a nice, kind woman who wouldn't hurt a fly. The reality was far from it and was much, much darker than I had ever imagined.

Rahul began consoling me and rubbing my back, before giving me the half-empty can of his energy drink. A few seconds later, we resumed our walk.

"I'm short of words. Yes, I'm moving on from her. But there was still a part of me that had a soft spot for her. And why wouldn't it? We spent countless hours talking with each other, the way she used to pounce on me whenever we met... I truly felt I was special. And now..." I couldn't continue speaking.

I felt as if I was going to faint right in front of him. We stopped walking and sat down on the bench again.

I continued, "She showed me the most beautiful dreams. Hundreds of them. I somehow believed that we were destined to be together. Back in the late 90s, I used to live in a building called Siddharth Apartment. It was right outside your area. Lieshaa and I had lived so close to each other for years and then finally met when you and I were in engineering. It made me believe that we had a past connection for a reason and were meant to be together."

"Siddharth Apartment?" he asked. His eyes widened.

"Yeah, why?"

He chuckled. "That was the apartment I caught her in, back in 2009. So, the two of you ARE connected, just not in the way you had imagined. Imagine how I must be feeling, realizing that I used to be out there working tirelessly, while the two of you... I still regret that you didn't tell me about it sooner."

"I had no idea you were planning to have another child. She later informed me and said that you and her grandmother were forcing her to have a kid," I told him.

"WHAT? HELL NO!" he exclaimed. "There are laws against these things. You just can't force a woman to have a kid. It was her decision. I mean, I wanted one as well, and it was a mutual decision. She lied to you again. Maybe she knew you weren't going to give her one and then made the decision. I have seen those messages where she begged you to give her a kid," Rahul said, leaving me dumbfounded.

"So, yeah. I think I should leave now. I'll say it again. It's not too late. Find someone. Someone you can trust. Someone who won't play with you the way she did. I love my kids and they need their mom. I don't have a choice. But you still do. Remember my words, Abhilash," he said, before taking out the moped's key out of his pocket.

"I will forever be indebted to you for this," I said while hugging him. "I'm sorry. I can't reverse what has happened, but I truly regret every bit of it."

"It's fine. You make sure you find someone who's trustworthy. And trust me, you're better off without her. You've dodged a bullet. If you had somehow managed to take her away, you would have been cheated on as well, somewhere down the line. Trust me. I know her better than anyone in the world."

"Yeah. After what you told me tonight, I don't doubt that one bit," I said.

"Rahul, one more thing," I exclaimed, while he was about to start his moped.

"Yeah. What happened?"

"I have a question that's been bothering me for a while now. You threatened the guys who pursued her. You even beat some of them up. I did way worse than any of them... I almost took her away from you. You could've done to me what you did to those guys, but you didn't. You didn't lay a finger on me. Instead, you came to meet me and told me the truth. You tried to help me. Why?"

He smiled at me.

"There were many reasons. Those texts... you rejected her advances in the beginning. You told her she was your friend's wife and what she wanted you to do was wrong. You only folded when she brought up her deceased mom and swore on her that she truly loved you. And then she told you that she had written her number in your book that you didn't see for five years. It put an idea in your mind that you were destined to be together. You left your job for her that you had been pursuing for a year or so, which meant you truly loved her and didn't just want to have fun with her like many others did in the past.

"Also, be it in engineering or recent years, you've always helped me. You loaned me your laptop. You offered to give me money during the pandemic. You agreed to become a witness when I needed those documents following my parents' passing. You aren't a bad person, you just believed the lies of a woman who isn't what she pretends to be.

"In the beginning, she probably would have run away with you. She proposed the idea to you. You rejected it. By the time you were ready to take her away, you were old news to her. Now imagine... what would have happened if you had managed to take her away back in 2018? She would have gotten bored of you as well, months down the line. I'm sure of that. And then, she would have cheated on you too. I actually feel bad for you. But thankfully, it's not late for you," he said, before extending his hand towards mine.

We shook hands before he rode away, his moped disappearing at a corner.

I began walking towards my home, pondering everything that had happened over the past 11 years.

It was all over. The nightmare that had been haunting me for the past two years was finally over. Rahul's words were ringing in my ears. The woman I once loved was nowhere close to what she pretended to be for years on end. The realization that I had lived a lie for four straight years had messed me up like nothing else ever did.

It wasn't going to be easy for me to come to terms with the fact that the future Lieshaa had promised me was never going to come to fruition. Everything we had dreamed of doing together for the rest of our lives was forever going to remain a pipe dream. Instead, she would be doing all of those things with Rahul till the very end. All I could do to feel better was to convince myself that she would've cheated on me as well somewhere down the line.

Despite what Lieshaa did, I hadn't lost faith. I still believed that I was going to find someone someday.

I had done something incredibly horrible. One of the most evil sins a man could commit. I betrayed a friend who trusted me. And it didn't take long before I paid a heavy price. A pain that persisted for two long years. And I still hadn't fully healed. Probably never would.

But it was time to move on. Move on from Lieshaa. Move on from the suffering that she had caused. A year ago, I was on the verge of suicide. Now, I was full of hope, and looking forward to the future. Looking forward to new challenges and experiences that were ahead of me. Looking forward to a new beginning.

But no matter what, a part of me would always cherish every single one of Lieshaa's lies till my last breath.

Those lies once made me happy. Gave me hope. Made me believe.

Those wicked, diabolical, and yet beautiful lies.

Epilogue

August 6, 2024, 11:20 p.m.

"I'm outside your building," I texted Shikha.

"What? Are you serious?" I instantly received a response.

"Yeah... we can meet if you want. I'm about to leave in a few minutes."

"Coming in 2, don't go!"

It had been a little over a month since I met Shikha. But why was I outside her apartment at 11:20 in the night?

This story truly began about two years ago.

I was a massive cricket fan in the early 2000s. I had stopped watching the sport in 2007, on the very day India got kicked out of the Cricket World Cup. In late 2022, I began watching cricket again. It had been about seven months since Lieshaa dumped me and my depression had gotten worse by that point.

I was yearning for something to keep me occupied and stumbled upon a T20 match between India and Australia shortly before the 2022 World Cup. And just like that, I was hooked again! Two massive heartbreaks followed, with India losing the semifinals of the 2022 T20 Cricket World Cup and the finals of the 2023 ODI Cricket World Cup.

Fast forward to June 29, 2024.

I was in a dilemma. India was all set to battle South Africa in the finals of the 2024 T20 Cricket World Cup at the Kensington Oval in Bridgetown, Barbados. I was wondering if I should watch the game at home or watch it in a public setting.

I had seen about a dozen live matches at cricket stadiums in the past, but never on a large screen at a restaurant/club. It was something I had been wanting to experience for quite some time and there couldn't have been a better occasion than the much-anticipated final between India and South Africa.

After contemplating for a while, I decided to head over to a popular food court in the city.

Sometimes, a person doesn't have the slightest idea that the decision they're making will end up being a life-changing one.

This was one of those decisions.

India won the toss while I was midway. Surprisingly, the adjoining parking lot was almost empty. I quickly parked the car at a corner and headed to the food court. I was expecting it to be jam-packed with people. To my utter delight, it was empty as well, but I could see people coming in one after the other.

The food court was an open area. There were about seven eateries on both sides. The large campus in the middle had a tiny playground for kids, tons of randomly placed tables and chairs, a bunch of trees, and a MASSIVE screen at the very end. I sprinted towards the first row. A large table, surrounded by six empty chairs, was all for the taking. I quickly sat down on one of the chairs. The rest were empty but weren't going to remain unoccupied for long. The screen was a few feet ahead of me and I knew right away that this was going to be an incredible viewing experience.

Finally, the match kicked off!

I managed to stay quiet for the first couple of overs. Then, I began cheering, oohing, and aahing on every single ball, LOUDLY, like many others around me were doing.

I was so engrossed in the game that I didn't even notice that a bunch of people had taken the rest of the chairs surrounding the table.

I smiled and nodded at the girl who had grabbed the chair beside mine. She smiled as well in response, before putting her focus on the screen.

"You aren't alone here, are you?" she asked me during a commercial.

"I am, actually. It's better to watch such a huge game in this setting rather than being cooped up at home. What about you? You're with them, right?" I pointed at the group of guys and girls who had taken the rest of the seats.

"Nah! I'm in the same boat as you. Didn't want to watch the game at home and decided to come here. I often visit the food court to grab a bite and wanted to see how it feels to watch a game on this massive screen," she said while pointing at the screen.

"I'm Abhilash, by the way," I said, extending my hand.

"Shikha," she replied, as she shook my hand firmly.

A few hours passed.

We were witnessing an instant classic. I, like many other guys nearby, was on the verge of tears. It had been 13 long years since India had won the Cricket World Cup. We were so close to finally tasting gold again. And then, Heinrich Klassen smashed 24 off Axar Patel's over.

South Africa now needed 30 off 30!

I bowed my head down in silence. I didn't feel like looking at the screen. With six wickets remaining and a required run-rate of six, there was no chance the Proteas were losing this one.

I suddenly felt a gentle pat on my back.

"You okay?" Shikha asked.

"I think I'm gonna leave. Can't watch the team choke another tournament," I said, putting the phone in my pocket and getting up.

"WHAT? It isn't over until the last ball is bowled! There's still a chance," she exclaimed.

"At this stage? AT 30 OFF 30?" I asked and chuckled at her.

"How about one more over? And then you leave if you still want to? Deal?" she put her hand forward.

That was when I FINALLY took a good look at her. For the past three hours or so, I was so absorbed in the game that I didn't pay much heed to her.

Until now. And she was a sight to behold.

She was petite and looked insanely fit. It was evident from her lean and toned physique that she hit the gym regularly. Her skin had a glow which seemingly was a result of regular workouts and a balanced diet. Her glistening, black eyes were captivating me to no end. She wore a gray T-shirt and dark blue jeans that fit her to a T.

It felt as if I was in a trance. My hand instinctively moved forward to shake hers while I smiled at her, before taking my seat.

Jasprit Bumrah gave a measly four runs in the next over, and so did Hardik Pandya, who took a wicket as well. Klassen was GONE! The 18th over, bowled by Bumrah, consisted of two runs and a wicket!

20 off 12!

We were suddenly back in the game! The atmosphere in the packed food court was electric! Every dot ball resulted in LOUD cheers and quick 10-second celebrations, with people jumping around, dancing, and screaming at the top of their lungs. The hardcore fan within me was going bananas as the climax was inching closer with each delivery.

I was looking at her after every delivery, excitedly telling her how many balls were left, as if the massive TV screen wasn't right in front of her. She couldn't stop laughing at the sudden change in my demeanor. Mere minutes ago, I was numb as a statue. Now, I couldn't help but jump around and hug fellow fans around me after every successful delivery.

The final over was here.

16 off 6.

Wicket off the first delivery! SKY's catch at the boundary! One of the greatest catches I had ever witnessed. Did he just catch the T20 World Cup?

16 off 5.

The second one went for a four. Absolute silence in the food court. You could cut the tension with a knife.

12 off 4.

A bye. Nothing to worry about.

11 off 3!

A leg bye! Another run! No big deal. We were inching closer to our first World Cup victory in 13 years!

10 off 2!

Hardik bowled a wide! The crowd collectively gasped.

9 off 2!

SKY took another catch! Barring another extra, this cup was OURS!

9 OFF 1!

Single!

JUST A SINGLE!

We had won!

WE HAD WON!

AFTER 13 LONG YEARS, WE WERE WORLD CHAMPIONS AGAIN!

The crowd erupted into cheers. People were overwhelmed with joy. Some were in tears. I was screaming, jumping, and hugging everyone in sight. I was incredibly close to leaving the court and missing this historic moment! If it hadn't been for Shikha, I would be at my home, banging my head against a wall for leaving early.

Where was she anyway?

Her chair was empty. I had begun celebrating with everyone as soon as the final ball was bowled, and now I couldn't find her.

Did she immediately leave without even saying a word? I didn't even know her full name! Why would she leave without at least saying goodbye?

And then I felt a pat on my back.

"I was grabbing a bottle of water. You want some?" She asked, pointing at one of the eateries on the right. "What did I say about the game not being over till the last ball is bowled?"

"Holy shit, you scared me! I thought you had left!" I said while taking a sip of water. "Do you live nearby?"

"God, I'm so sorry, I didn't mean to scare you. Yeah, I live about three km from here. I took a cab here 'cause my moped was in the repair center. Searching for one now," she said, taking out her phone.

"Would you mind if I drop you, Shikha?" I hesitatingly asked. It took every ounce of courage within me to ask the question.

"Umm... you sure you're not in a hurry to go back?" she asked.

"Absolutely not. I have all the time in the world," I excitedly said, before asking her to follow me to the parking lot.

On our way, we saw people lighting firecrackers, dancing on the roads and the streets, blowing horns, and even distributing sweets.

As we were about to reach her home, it started raining heavily. I made sure to drop her right in front of the gate of her apartment.

"What a night, huh? We should do this again sometime," I finally gave her a hint in a playful manner.

"Absolutely! But that would require you to take my number, haha!"

I breathed a sigh of relief and handed over my phone to her.

"I'll call you in an hour or so?" I asked her while unlocking the door.

"Or sooner, if you wish!" she said, giggling at me.

She finally left the car and sprinted towards the elevator. I drove away immediately after, wanting to reach home quickly and call her ASAP.

That night, we talked for about two hours straight. We then decided to meet up for coffee in a day or two. The two of us immediately hit it off and started dating less than a week after our first meeting.

Everything had happened so fast. I was genuinely happy for the first time in two years. Before I met Shikha, I couldn't get past a day without thinking about Lieshaa and her betrayal. Now, I could feel Lieshaa's thoughts slowly fading away into nothingness with each passing day. The smile on my face hadn't been this genuine in ages.

I was content.

It was refreshing being with someone like Shikha after the disaster of a relationship I had with Lieshaa.

The only similarity between Lieshaa and Shikha was that both of them treated me in the early stages like I was the last man on earth. Barring that, Shikha wasn't anything like Lieshaa.

Lieshaa liked playing mind games. Shikha HATED manipulation.

Lieshaa used to bring up her exes and other guys to make me feel insecure. Shikha never once mentioned an ex.

Lieshaa used to change topics and ignore questions during fights, which annoyed me to no end. Shikha preferred talking things out over staying silent and harming the relationship further.

Lieshaa pretended to care. Shikha actually seemed to care.

Lieshaa lied, A LOT. She had told me so many lies over the years that I ended up writing a book based on them. Shikha liked being honest, transparent, and even blunt if needed.

Lieshaa had convinced me that she was never going to leave me, no matter what. She had a way with words that could convince any man that she had eyes only for him.

She had managed to make a mockery out of my love and trust. I didn't want to end up looking like a clown twice in a row and was treading lightly with Shikha.

There's this saying I had read years ago somewhere.

"Hurt people hurt people."

When a person gets betrayed after being promised eternal love, it tends to change them for the worse. While I showered Lieshaa with the utmost respect and admiration from the get-go, I wasn't treating Shikha the same way.

I would occasionally lie to her without feeling guilty. I would try to gaslight her into thinking that she was the problem in case we fought. I would get mad at her for the most ridiculous reasons. The littlest of mistakes would get on my nerves.

If she took time to respond, I would get mad. If she didn't call me at least twice a day, I would get mad. If she missed a call of mine, I would get mad.

Once an incredibly caring and loving person, I had now turned into a toxic and miserable being. There was a reason why I had told Lieshaa that she was way deadlier than her husband who resorted to violence against guys who pursued her. Lieshaa's lies were still affecting me and my personal life, months after I saw her last. I was taking out my frustration and anger on someone who had absolutely nothing to do with what had happened in my past.

And it was not fair to Shikha in the least.

I was trying my very best to treat her with nothing but love and affection. Unfortunately, the toxic side of me was coming out every other day and she was slowly reaching her breaking point.

Shikha was doing everything in her power to make the relationship work while I was unintentionally trying to ruin it. She was patient with me whereas any other woman in her place would have bailed, and understandably so.

Every person has a breaking point, though, and she finally reached hers one day.

"I'm sorry, but I can't do this anymore." She wrote. "I can't go on like this. I've tried, but I simply can't. My mental health is going to shit."

"What? You're ending it?" I asked.

"Yeah, it's over. Lose my number, please," she replied bluntly.

I blocked her immediately. Everywhere. The toxic asshole in me was too proud and angry to talk things out with her and try to be better.

A couple of days later, I received a text from her. These were her exact words:

"I'm sorry. I overreacted. Missing you badly. Give me one chance, that's all I'm asking. I'm an emotional mess. I'm not eating properly. I'm not getting enough sleep. I break down every other hour, realizing that it's over between us. Can we talk for a minute, Abhilash?"

She didn't overreact. At all. She had endured my toxicity for weeks on end before finally snapping at me and leaving for her own good. But she was still trying to be the bigger person and accepting a mistake that didn't exist.

I blocked her number as well.

My toxicity had gotten the best of me, to the point that I was happy with losing the best thing to have ever happened to me.

That night, I went out for dinner with a couple of friends. While returning, we decided to have *paan* (betel leaf) at a popular kiosk, which happened to be in the same area as Shikha's apartment. In fact, her apartment was not more than 100 meters from the kiosk.

After finishing our *paans*, we headed back to the car that we had parked on the opposite side of the road. While my friends were casually talking with each other as we approached the car, a storm was going on in my mind.

"She lives right behind that building in the corner," I told my friends. I had already told them about what had happened between Shikha and me while we were heading to the restaurant.

"What? You wanna talk to her or something?"

"Nah! She decided to end it. I'll respect it," I said and sneered, recalling how she was begging me to take her back mere hours ago.

I could see a part of the building she lived in from where we stood. She was probably in her room at that moment, dejected, miserable, and full of regrets.

The way I once was, not too long ago.

Back in 2022, I was betrayed by someone I believed was the love of my life. Someone I trusted with every fiber of my being. Over the next two years, I saw a side of her that I didn't even know existed. It later dawned on me that this was her true self, and the kind, pure-hearted, loving face I had grown to love was merely a mask to hide the horror that lay underneath.

After dumping me, Lieshaa repeatedly made it known that I meant absolutely nothing to her. It was as if she was an entirely different person.

"And Abhilash... if you leave me someday, or stop talking to me for some reason, I won't be able to live. I can't help it. My heart... it won't be able to bear the pain."

"Dude, I have a family... why are you creating problems? Why are you trying to destroy my family dude? My brother's here for a few days, and you... why are you forcing me? You're destroying my family... shit!"

I had seen the best of her and the worst of her.

To my horror, the worst of her was her actual, true self, which she had somehow managed to hide from me for years on end.

Lieshaa was the most dangerous person, woman or man, that I had ever met.

She had the power to ruin anybody without ever lifting a finger on them. After she left me, I kept pleading with her to keep her promises and take me back. Her heart had suddenly turned into stone, and she couldn't care less about the person she once couldn't live without. While I wept for her every day, she casually went on with her life without an ounce of compassion for me. That's the kind of cruel, wicked, and despicable woman she was.

And at that moment, there wasn't a shred of difference between Lieshaa and me. I was as cruel, wicked, and despicable as her.

I had blocked Shikha, wasn't responding to her messages, and had completely cut her out of my life. I showed no compassion when she texted me, trying to make things right and get back together. While she was crying uncontrollably, I was enjoying a hearty meal with my friends with no remorse in my heart.

The past two years flashed in front of my eyes in a matter of seconds.

I recalled how Lieshaa enjoyed hundreds of such meals with her family with no remorse in her heart while I wept for her. For two years.

I recalled how badly it hurt.

The pain I went through, the suffering I endured, the way I longed for the presence of the woman who had stopped loving me for good. I wouldn't wish that on my worst enemy.

And now, I had become the very person that I hated with all my heart. I was putting Shikha through the torment I was once subjected to.

This wasn't me. I wasn't Lieshaa.

I wasn't someone who would promise all the love in the world to a person and snatch it all away in an instant, leaving them dead inside. I wasn't someone who would put a person through hell when all they did was love me with all their heart.

"I'll come back in a minute," I said to my friends while heading towards her building.

"Where are you off to?" one of my friends asked.

"To make things right," I said, with a big smile on my face, while pointing at her home. My friends smiled at me as well, realizing that I had decided to meet her.

"I'm outside your building," I texted her.

"What? Are you serious?"

"Yeah... we can meet if you want. I'm about to leave in a few minutes."

"Coming in two, don't go please!"

I began walking towards her apartment, my eyes pinned to the gate. A few seconds later, she appeared at the gate and quickly walked through it, having noticed me in the distance.

She came running before stopping right in front of me.

"I'm terribly sor--"

I immediately put my hand over her mouth, before locking her in a tight embrace.

She didn't need to apologize for not wanting to put up with my abusive behavior. The toxicity within me had to end. The mind games, the manipulation, the silent treatment, the blaming, the occasional lies.

All of it had to end.

I was not going to do to Shikha what Lieshaa had done to me.

I was never going to hurt her again.

The End

Behind

Believe

Believe:

12 Blunt Lessons

Karma eventually hits you back

Ideally, Abhilash should've blocked Lieshaa immediately after learning that she was into him. He didn't. Instead, He let her coax him into reciprocating her love and eventually fell for her.

Lieshaa's love made him betray his friend's trust. He had committed an unforgivable sin and it didn't take long before karma came to collect the debt. He almost ended his life after suffering for more than a year.

Karma is real. And the suffering it will inflict on you could be a million times worse than what you've inflicted on someone else.

If they often suspect you of cheating on them, they are likely projecting

Lieshaa used to fear that Abhilash was talking to other women and possibly cheating on her. There were many occasions when he sent her screenshots of his conversations with other people to convince her that he was faithful to her.

And then he found a message sent by a guy that she had saved on her phone. Three years later, after he was dumped, she revealed that she had feelings for another guy.

Lieshaa was projecting.

Some people use defense mechanisms to deal with stressful thoughts or guilt and end up accusing others of things that they've done.

She was most certainly feeling guilty of cheating on Abhilash and decided to cope with it by accusing him of cheating on her.

No matter how trustworthy they seem to be, never fully trust someone

You're bound to come across genuine, good-hearted people. But there's always a chance that the one promising you the world has ulterior motives in mind.

Lieshaa swore on her deceased mom that she and Abhilash were meant for each other. And that they were going to be together forever.

Now? She wakes up every day, looks in the mirror with zero remorse or guilt, and is probably sending a text to someone else, swearing on her mom that she and him are made for each other.

Never trust someone fully. NEVER.

They aren't busy, they've just gotten bored of you

After Lieshaa threw Abhilash out of her life, he tried to get her back on multiple occasions. She was busy. She was sick. She was loaded with work. Rahul was nearby. And the list goes on...

Excuses.

When Lieshaa contacted him in 2018, he was new and exciting. He was someone that she wanted all for herself. At any cost.

She used to be busy. She used to get sick. She used to be loaded with work. Rahul used to be nearby. But it never stopped her from texting Abhilash all the time.

Once they start ignoring you, DON'T believe their excuses. They're taking the easy way out and avoiding conflict by making excuses. It's time to accept the bitter truth that they aren't yours anymore.

Evil people have two faces and you will eventually see the hidden one

In the beginning, when Lieshaa was desperate to make Abhilash hers, she acted and presented herself like the most innocent being he had ever seen. Someone too pure and wholesome for this world.

After she was done with him and didn't need to put on a mask anymore, her real self became visible to him. This woman was nowhere close to the kind-hearted, gentle soul he had met years ago. She was cold, apathetic, and didn't have a shred of compassion in her heart.

What hurt him the most was that she had most certainly put on the mask again for someone else, someone new, someone who excited her like he did once. The idea that she was making the same promises to someone else, texting him every night, possibly meeting him, broke Abhilash from within.

If they're cheating with you on someone, they WILL cheat on you with someone

Lieshaa cheated on her husband with Abhilash. He betrayed his friend Rahul after falling in love with his wife. He should've realized that he could end up taking Rahul's place somewhere down the line.

And he did.

Her promises seemed too real. Her assurances were too convincing. When a person swears on their deceased mom that she will love you till her last breath, you can't help but believe them. Abhilash did too and paid a heavy price for his delusion. She ended up falling for someone else. At least two other guys, to the best of his knowledge.

They will lie to you while looking straight into your eyes and with zero remorse

When Abhilash found out that Lieshaa had saved a text from a guy in her Notes app, he confronted her. She cried relentlessly until he had to tell her that he believed her.

When Rahul showed her the pictures she had clicked with Abhilash, she looked him in the eye and told him that they were photoshopped.

When Abhilash confronted her at her home, she straight up told him that he was the one who always used to force her to come to meet him. If he hadn't saved their texts, she could've done irreparable damage to him in more ways than one.

Evil people will lie to your face without a shred of guilt or regret in their hearts.

In their most vulnerable moments, evil people will do everything in their power to save themselves and put the blame on others. They WILL lie through their teeth.

Evil beings don't shy away from contradicting themselves if it benefits them in any manner

When Lieshaa wanted Abhilash, he rejected her and told her that she was married to Rahul and had a family. Her response?

"Then why should we even talk? That's wrong as well, right?

Four years later, when she was done playing with him, this was what she said when he asked her to come back:

"I have a family. A husband. A kid."

Inherently evil people will contradict themselves as and when it suits their needs. They won't feel the tiniest bit of shame while doing so.

When you truly love someone, you ignore every single red flag

Lieshaa used to bring up other guys to see how Abhilash would react. She often used to suspect that he was pursuing other women. She lied to him on several occasions

He ignored every single red flag.

When you are in love with someone and don't want to lose them at any cost, you tend to ignore their wrongdoings. All of them.

If they ignore you and come running to you ONLY when they need help, RUN… and don't look back

Lieshaa left Abhilash's text unread a few months after dumping him. Five months later, she contacted him out of the blue and asked for monetary help right away.

No apologies or regrets for treating him like he didn't matter to her. The only thought she had in her mind was that this clown was still madly in love with her and would still help her after what she did.

If a person does this, they are as evil as they come and are devoid of empathy. RUN away from them for your own good. They will not add any value to your life.

After Abhilash didn't give her the money, he knew that their story was truly finished. It was finished months ago, but she had hoped that he was still of some use to her.

When she learned that he wasn't, she didn't have any reason to talk to him. He knew at that very moment that she was never going to call him, send a text, or meet him again.

Think of your loved ones if you ever feel like ending your life over lost love

At one point, Abhilash had fallen in love with Lieshaa to such an extent that he used to have the most ridiculous thoughts.

"If the time comes, I will gladly give my life for her," he used to say to himself.

When she left him crying, he came incredibly close to putting an end to his life. He had zero concern for his family, his blood, who had been by his side during this ordeal. He didn't care about what would happen to them after he took his life.

Only when he saw someone else taking their own life and leaving their family destroyed beyond repair, he realized his mistake.

If you ever feel suicidal over someone who doesn't care, remember that you need to live for someone who does.

At the end of the day, inner beauty is what matters the most

They can be the most beautiful person to ever exist. They can have insanely pretty eyes. Their skin can be white as snow. And none of it will matter if they aren't loving, compassionate, and kind to you.

Lieshaa was insanely pretty. She also convinced Abhilash that she was the nicest, most caring, and soft-hearted woman he had ever come across.

The moment he confronted her at her home and she lied that he was the one who used to force her to come and meet him, something struck his mind.

He looked at her and saw the ugliest person to ever exist on the planet.

She still looked good on the outside. But to him, at that very moment, she was the most hideous being he had ever laid his eyes on.

As they say, beauty is temporary, but character is permanent.

Gallery

Note: If you haven't read *Believe* yet, it's advisable to avoid going through this section. It contains massive spoilers from the novel and will ruin the entire story for you!

The following pages feature photographs of notable real-life locations, objects, and exchanges from the story, *Believe*. The faces of people who appear in the photographs have been censored to protect anonymity.

Every photograph featured in this section has been clicked by the author.

A college building is visible in the distance from the terrace of Abhilash's home. The woman who was the inspiration behind the character of Lieshaa attended 12th grade in this building. It's also the spot in front of which Abhilash used to occasionally pick Lieshaa up.

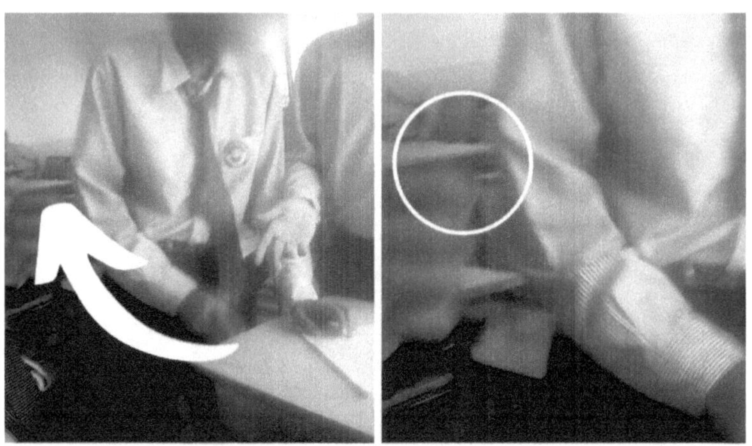

The picture shows the desk where the guys behind the characters of Rahul and Samay used to sit in college. This is the same desk beside which Rahul grabbed Ishan by the tie after he cracked a joke and mentioned his then-girlfriend, Lieshaa.

The circled area shows the spot where Abhilash used to park his bike. This is the same spot where Abhilash once stood when Lieshaa came to pick Rahul up and saw him for the first time.

The first picture shows the workshop that Rahul and Abhilash used to visit during the sixth semester. The workshop doesn't exist anymore and has been replaced with a shop where electrical appliances are repaired. The second picture shows the spot that housed a small coconut water kiosk 11 years ago. The same kiosk in front of which Lieshaa once sat on Rahul's bike, sipping coconut water and staring at Abhilash.

The picture shows the bookshelf from which Abhilash used to take out books for Lieshaa to read. The arrow points to the stack of books in which THAT book stood for five long years.

This is the book in question. The picture shows the cover of the book as well as the very first page. The areas where Lieshaa jotted down her cell number have been blurred.

The picture shows the road beside the back gate of Abhilash's college. The highlighted spot at the bottom was where Abhilash stood while handing over the assignment copy to Rahul. The highlighted spot at the top was where Rahul and Lieshaa stopped their moped and waited for Abhilash to come out, before heading towards him.

A slope is visible in the highlighted spot. This is the very spot where Lieshaa stood while Rahul was borrowing books from Abhilash in his home. A bunch of children were running around and playing right in front of her, on the road.

Final Selection Status

You are Selected for
1)MBA - TELECOM MANAGEMENT

Click here for Selected Call Letter

The screengrab shows the graphic Abhilash saw in the browser of his phone on the evening of February 28, 2014.

The first picture shows the campus where Abhilash lived for two years while pursuing an MBA. The hostel was about a 3-minute walk away from the spot featured in the picture. The second picture shows another view of the campus and was clicked from the second floor of Abhilash's college. A massive mountain is visible in the distance. The entire campus is situated on the top of a mountain on the outskirts of Pune.

The first picture was taken at 2:32 a.m. on May 27, 2018. Abhilash and his brother were on their way to the airport to take a flight to UAE. Lieshaa was most certainly asleep at her home about a km away, with Abhilash having had no thought of her for about five years at that point. A little over two months later, she would contact Abhilash on Facebook. The second picture was taken at 2:33 a.m. on July 17, 2022, on the very same road. Abhilash and his brother were on their way to the airport to catch a flight to Sharjah again, from where they would catch another flight to Cairo, Egypt.

The picture was taken shortly after Abhilash and his brother entered their hotel room in Dubai on May 27, 2018. About an hour later, they brought some food and soft drinks to the room. The drinks spilled inside the bag on the way to the hotel and the duo cleaned up the round table shown in the picture, before eating the soggy food. It was a small nuisance that later turned into an incredibly precious memory for Abhilash.

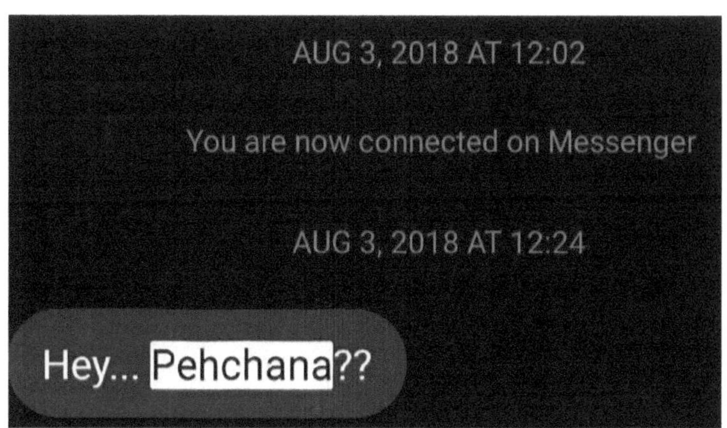

Minutes after the clock struck 12 on August 3, 2018, Abhilash received a text. He had accepted Lieshaa's friend request 22 minutes ago. The message read "Hey... Remember me??" (translated). Abhilash's normal, untroubled, drama-free life took a sudden turn at this very moment, and it would never be the same again.

I think one of the saddest things is when two people really get to know each other: their secrets, their fears, their favourite things, what they love, what they hate, literally everything, and then they go back to being strangers. It's like you have to walk past them and pretend like you never knew them, never even talked to them before, when really, you know everything about them.

The picture that Lieshaa sent Abhilash when his hectic schedule was making it hard for him to respond to her texts during his short-lived run as a rural banker. He ended up leaving the bank for her sake. Four years later, Abhilash sent the same image to Lieshaa. There was no response.

The first picture shows the government bank where Abhilash worked for about a month in September 2018. It was located about 150 km from his hometown in Central India. The second picture shows Abhilash heading to the bank on the very first day of his job. The car got into a "traffic jam" for about 20 minutes on its way to the bank.

The picture shows the apartment where Abhilash lived in the late 90s after moving to the city. Lieshaa lived less than 500 m from his home. This was seemingly the same apartment building where Rahul caught Lieshaa with a guy, almost a decade after Abhilash's family left it.

The first picture shows the spot where Abhilash picked Lieshaa up on his bike on the evening of January 4, 2019. It was their very first meeting. The second picture shows a hospital complex situated on the opposite side of the road, where Abhilash saw a psychiatrist in hopes of curing his depression in mid-2022.

The picture that Abhilash took after reaching his hotel room in Egypt. He and his brother had traveled to Egypt in an attempt to cure his depression.

The picture shows the ring that Abhilash had bought from Egypt in hopes of winning Lieshaa back as he was aware that she loved jewelry. Lieshaa was about one month pregnant with her second child while he was buying the ring for her.

The picture that Abhilash took from the rooftop of the tallest building in Bangkok, Thailand. Solo travel had been on his bucket list for a while at that point. While gazing at the incredible Bangkok skyline and taking it all in, Abhilash was fully aware that his life was about to come to an end in a matter of months.

WWE legend and Hollywood actor John Cena getting ready to wrestle in India for the first time in his illustrious career. Abhilash had destroyed his suicide letter mere days before the event.

The scenes at a food court on the night of June 29, 2024. The first picture shows the crowd looking at the massive screen, fully prepared for what was about to come. The second picture shows the exact moment India won the T20 World Cup by defeating South Africa in the finals.